amboi

amboi

ANDI GUIMONT

Palmetto Publishing Group
Charleston, SC

Amboi
Copyright © 2019 by Andi Guimont

First Edition

Printed in the United States

ISBN-13: 978-1-64111-405-9
ISBN-10: 1-64111-405-3

chapter 1

I'm standing in my kitchen watching my daughter leave for school. Coffee in hand, I go to my bathroom to get ready for work. I start to dream back to my first husband and our kids. When I was Amanda Hugh, maiden name Bittle. Married to Max Hugh for sixty-eight years. Died at the age of eighty-nine. Amboi.

Amogny (*Ah-mog-knee*) is the mediator of sorts in the Amboi world. He helps the transitions between lives go smoother, and even explains to newcomers what is going on. The only thing different between us and humans is that we live several lives. How many lives we have is unique to each Amboi.

I think about my past family as I do my hair and make-up. I had three children: Charlotte, Rose, and Peter Hugh.

Though I loved my family so dearly, I find it hard to hold on to those feelings of love. Amogny said that I would lose feelings for those of past lives, some Amboi faster than others. I have yet to meet another Amboi. Amogny said there aren't a lot of Amboi in the world, and we are spread throughout.

I listen to Garrett stir at the sound of his alarm clock to bring me back to this life, where I am Amanda Kramer, forty-five, married to Garrett Kramer, forty-seven, for twenty-one years. Where I am brunette not blond, chubby not thin, and a few inches taller, with brown eyes instead of blue.

"Babe, your alarm clock." I poke at him.

"I know," he grumbles, mocking sadness.

Though only a half hour, we make the most of our mornings together. We get ready for work by kissing as we move by each other in the bathroom, or while passing out clothes from the closet, firing sassy comments as we go. Soon I am out the door, coffee in hand, and off to work.

Roger's law firm is a short drive from my house. I walk in and settle into my space before greeting everybody. The lawyers are having a morning meeting that seems to have been going on for a while now. Feeling that everyone could use new drinks, I make my rounds. Two lattes, a smoothie, and muffin later, everyone looks like their spirits have lifted a little. Feeling as though I've done my good deed for the day, I go back to my desk. The meeting wraps up shortly, and everyone makes a break for their offices—everyone except Mary.

"Ugh, thanks for the muffin. Saved my life." She huffs while laying across my desk dramatically.

"Sure, no problem. So what was up with the meeting, anyways?"

She rolls her eyes. "Boss man is hiring someone new and wants us to play nice." She pauses, then says, "Oh yeah, he is making him partner."

I practically feel my mouth fall to the ground. "What? Who? Why?"

"Not sure. I will feel it out today, though, and let you know at lunch."

And with that she's off.

I greet customers and point them in the directions they need to go while reading through emails from Brynn's school. Part of me wishes I had sent her to the private school my other children went to. I know that Charlotte and Rose would never meet her, but I want the homey feeling just the same. However, I was not born in New York this time. I was born in Texas, and Evangel Christian school is too far to send Brynn.

Living in this second life I found myself to be a lot more free-spirited. I'm not so afraid. Still too overbearing, Brynn would tease. Rose grew to resent me for the way I parented in my late life. When she had her own children and moved away, she thought my methods harsh. Learning from my mistakes in the first life, I loosened up with Brynn. Let her go out with her friends and party, even. Charlotte would praise me for taking positive steps forward. For opening my mind. Was I so terrible to them? Finding myself lost in thoughts of my past life again, I switch to reading the gossip email thread about the new partner being brought in.

By the time lunch rolls around, everyone has guesses. Some guess a family member, or childhood friend. Some go as far to say it's his wife bitching about not being "showcased" enough. I sit with Mary and Cindy and eavesdrop on people's conversations, and we make snide remarks to each other.

"Sorry, Lynda, but no one cares about the color your cat threw up today," Cindy mumbles to us.

"Really, though, that has to be fake, right?" Mary asks, looking up from her phone. " I mean, really brown, green, yellow; today is a light red. What's tomorrow? A light purple?"

We snicker at the sarcastic remark and then dive into our own conversation. "So, Brynn is going to a party tomorrow," I say as if I just told her secret.

"How's Momma Bear doing with that?" Cindy asks.

"I'm okay with it. She is seventeen, after all. I feel it's about time." Something on my face tells them I'm lying.

"Just knowing it in your head is different than feeling it," Mary states.

"I know. She is seventeen. I should be fine with this, right? All kids go to parties, and she is responsible. Still, I've been young." *Twice.* "And I know what young men think."

"Just let her go. Have a date night with Garrett tomorrow," Mary says, still trying to convince my racing heart.

———

Hours later, Brynn is working on homework while I make dinner. Garrett comes stomping in the house. "I can't wait to retire."

He plops down on the couch and turns the TV on but the volume low. "Smells good, honey," he says, half sarcastic.

"Wait until you taste it. I think you'll like this one."

He takes his shoes off and walks over to where I'm cooking. He opens his mouth and makes a noise. Knowing he wants to taste it, I put a sample on his tongue. He makes a face, then drops his shoes by the door. I think I hear him whisper "bluh" under his breath. During dinner Garrett thanks me for cooking, and he and Brynn offer to clean up. We share about our days and plans we have for the weekend. Brynn and I are going shopping for jewelry tomorrow while Garrett golfs with his work friends, then we are going to have a dinner party while Brynn is off at her party. On Sunday we are going to church, and then spending the day together doing family activities.

"I got accepted to the University of Texas today." Brynn beams.

Garrett and I sling compliments at her.

"Oh, wow! I knew you would."

"Congrats, honey! I'm proud of you."

She looks overjoyed with our praise, and continues eating her spaghetti.

"Any ideas what you are going for yet?" Garret asks.

Garrett and I ask her this about every other week to emphasize that she needs to pick something, and before school starts.

She rolls her eyes. "No, I still don't know. Can't I do my generals and then see what I'd like to decide then?"

"Well, how would you know what classes to take the first year if you don't even know what you are studying?" Garrett doesn't let up that easy.

Brynn shoots me a pleading gaze to step in before he goes any farther, and they start fighting again. "Brynn," I interject. "That sounds like an okay idea. Just make sure you take classes that can easily transfer to whatever field you would want."

Garrett looks like he isn't done speaking on the matter, but I know it will be a conversation for just the two of us tonight. We finish eating, and as promised, they do the cleaning.

"Cards?" Brynn asks.

"Sounds great." I smile.

We sit and play cards the rest of the evening, and Brynn tells us about her friend and the party tomorrow.

"Her name is Amber. Mom, you would really like her." She glances at me over her cards. "Anyways, her parents have a lot of money, I guess, and don't care that she throws parties. I promise to be home at an early time, and no drinking. Pinkie promise."

Garrett, not yet satisfied, says, "Well, be careful what you drink. If you don't know who gave you that drink, or where it came from, don't drink it. Don't go alone in a room with a guy, and call us if you feel the least bit uncomfortable."

Brynn and I share a glance, then burst into giggles. "Babe, the strict dad act is sexy on you."

"Groooooosssss," Brynn whines, and covers her ears. "Topic change, stat."

And just like that, it's Garretts turn to laugh at Brynn.

"All right, bed." I start picking up cards while they head to the bedrooms.

"Tonight was fun," Garrett says as we crawl under the covers.

"It's nice to have a kid that actually wants to be around us." A sadness washes over me as I think of Rose.

"You say that but look sad." Garrett is too observant.

How can I explain that I am just thinking about a daughter he's never known about, with a man who is long gone by now? Heck, even Rose and Peter could be gone by now. Sometimes I wish I was an Amboi who lost feelings from past lives faster. Then I wouldn't have to be so conscious about my face giving me away.

"Oh, I just hear stories from work about all the kids in the middle of divorce, and how they come to resent their parents, even if they are the one on the bad end of things. It's just disappointing how things work out sometimes." I roll away from him in hopes he won't catch my white lie.

"Well, try to leave work at work. Be glad we have a daughter who won't have to go through that, and who loves us as much as we love her." He snuggles up to my back in an attempt to comfort me.

What he doesn't realize is this earth-shattering thought: All three of my "AH" children are probably dead. Yes, I lost them, in a sense, when I died, but I never sat and thought about when they would die. They seemed happy, from what I could tell when I left them. All married with kids, but I didn't factor in the effect my death would have on them, and how they are today.

Around eleven the next morning, Brynn meets me in the kitchen, ready to go shopping.

"Give me two minutes to finish my coffee," I tell her.

She rolls her eyes, but agrees. We stop by the bakery and pick up some doughnuts for breakfast, then we are off to the local mall to get jewelry and maybe shoes. Brynn is controlling the radio while I drive. Her taste in music is terrible. Actually, a lot of music in this era is terrible. Some girl is singing about her big butt, and that's when I tell her to change the music to something appropriate. I am the cool parent, but even I have limits. The mall is not far out of town. I park as far from the building to get the most outside time I can. I also need to reach my step goal for the day.

"Do you ever even meet you step goal with your desk job and all?" Brynn asks when I get out of the car.

"Yes, I make sure to walk around and talk to all the lawyers. Even walk to lunch everyday with Mary." The break room isn't a far walk, but she doesn't need to know that. She also doesn't need to know that I lowered my step goal.

"I smell the white lie on you like bad perfume." She laughs.

I roll my eyes at her and chuckle too. We know this mall well. It's our favorite shopping spot, with all the shops we like all in one building. We go to the fashion jewelry store and pick out the perfect accessories for tonight's events. Brynn plans on wearing a burgundy shirt with a yellow plaid sweater, jeans, and beige ankle boots that I am letting her borrow. She picks out gold earrings and a matching ring set. I plan on wearing a gray T-shirt dress with leggings. I pick out a bold blue necklace to add color to the outfit, and find a large matching blue ring. Once we are both decided, I pay for the items, and we head out for lunch.

"What are you craving, hunny bunny?" I ask her.

"Tacos."

We drive to a fast food taco place and order to go. We get home just after three, and start to prepare for the evening. Brynn vacuums while Garrett does the dishes from today. I clean the living room and set the table with our nice dishes. It's just some work friends of Garrett's from his office, but they are all upper class, while we land about middle class. Not that Garrett doesn't make much money, we just spend it on doing things rather than living comfy. Much less so than in my old life. Max and I were set in a nice home. I didn't have to work, and stayed home with the kids. Max was often too busy to be around much. Garrett is home every night around five thirty. It's nice to have a husband who is around more, and sees me as a partner rather than a live-in nanny.

Garrett cooks dinner while I get ready. Brynn leaves just before our guests arrive.

"Bye, honey. Remember, home by midnight." I kiss her cheeks as she walks out the door.

"You look lovely," Garrett compliments her, and hugs her goodbye.

We close the door behind her and both head to the kitchen for a drink. After my glass of wine is poured and Garrett has a cup of Captain Cola, we settle at the table and wait for our guests. Just minutes later, there is a knock on the door. Behind it, a blonde woman, who introduces herself as Joelle. She and her husband Luke greet us. We exchange formalities as needed, and then get drinks for the newcomers.

"So what is your role at Ace, Luke?" I ask to make conversation, even though I already know he is the president of the company.

He dives into a story about how he started at entry level, and eventually turns it into a whole motivational speech about how anyone can make it in this country. I appreciate the excitement he holds for his job, even though he's a veteran at it. Joelle then takes the conversation and tells us about the vet clinic she owns in the next town over. After a few too many horror stories, the next guests arrive. This time it's Josh, Garretts co-VP, and his wife Rachel. Rachel opts not to drink, and Josh fills a half-full glass of rum before adding the soda. Rachels catches me watching him pour it, and gives me an apologetic and embarrassed look. I give her my best reassuring smile and lead the girls into the living room for pre-dinner chatter, while the guys hang back in the kitchen to finish dinner.

"Any recommendations for music?" I ask, even though music is already playing and I have no intention of changing it.

As we settle onto the couches, they both agree that what is playing is fine. Awkward glances are exchanged before

Rachel finally breaks the silence. "So what do you do for work, Amanda?"

"I am a secretary at a law firm, and how about you?" I ask to be polite.

"Oh, I'm a stay-at-home mom," she says, seeming embarrassed again. "How about you, Joelle?"

Happy to take control of the conversation, Joelle launches into telling more horror stories from the vet clinic. If only Mary and Cindy were here, we could at least make fun of her on Monday. Instead, I sit and try to feign interest as much as possible.

Garrett yells from the kitchen when dinner is done. Relieved, I get up with the girls and go to sit in the dining room. Ribs, salad, and vegetables are spread across the table. Glasses are refilled, and dinner begins with everyone eating too fast to talk. It's a nice silence, though, a break from the conversations that have been going on tonight. Rachel seems nice enough, but is too shy to say much. The guys mostly hold the conversation on work related topics, so there isn't much for us to interject with. Rachel offers to help me clean up once everyone is done eating. Joelle and the guys go back to the living room and turn on the TV.

"Thank you for dinner," Rachels squeaks.

"Garrett is the chef. If I tried to make this, you wouldn't be able to tell what you are eating."

She smiles. "You and Garrett are adorable. I noticed you exchanging loving glances during dinner."

Had we? "Thank you. You and Josh also seem like a lovely couple."

Her face goes dark, but she's back to smiling just as fast. "Yes, he is a wonderful husband."

Unsure how to continue this conversation, I walk to the kitchen with dirty dishes.

"Your home is lovely, by the way." Back to awkward small talk.

"You are too sweet." I smile back at her.

"You just have one daughter?" she asks.

"Yes, her name is Brynn. Do you and Josh have any kids?"

"Yes, we have two boys, Pete and Jake."

I can see in her eyes all the love she holds for her boys. Somewhere deep inside me, I know she is only with Josh today because of those boys.

"How old are they?" I ask.

As the conversation continues, I let my mind stray to when I met Amogny. When I died, I found myself in a dark room, standing on a floating platform, with three hallways sticking out on each side. Each door had a number posted on it. At the back of the half-circle platform was an archway with a throne of sorts. A man sat in the chair.

"I am Amogny." His voice was strained to sound deeper than it really was.

He stood in front of me in all his six-foot glory. His pale skin was only visible on the lower half of his face. The rest of his body was covered in black; a black robe with the hood covering half his face, and black gloves over his hands. I looked at his pointed nose peeking out under the hood.

"Um, where am I?" I noticed my voice didn't change in the after life.

"This is Amboi HQ. Listen, then ask questions," he ordered. "You are an Amboi. You have several lives. How many lives is unique to each Amboi. It's rumored that the universe gives you signs when your lives are low. No Amboi have supernatural talents. In fact, the only thing that separates you from a normal human is that you have several lives. On the bright side, most Amboi remember their past lives even in their new ones."

He paused, and gave me a quick glance from under the hood. I was able to notice that his eyes were dark green. "Questions?"

About a million. "Nope."

He seemed confused by this, but moved on anyways. "You can stay here for twenty-four human hours. Then you are kicked back to the human world, and reborn to a new family. You see six rooms. Even though you aren't in the human world, you still feel the effects, at least at first. You can sleep in room one. Room six is the women's bathroom, five is for the guys. All other rooms are for Amboi in transition to mingle."

I didn't take the time to mingle with the other Amboi. I jumped right into my next life. I was too freaked out by all this information. I wanted proof. I jumped in, and now had so many questions.

I realize that Rachel has caught on that I was paying attention. "Sorry," I mumble.

"No problem." She smiles sweetly. "Anyways, now that dishes are done, we should probably get going."

As if on cue, Josh gets up from the couch. "We should get going."

Joelle and Luke follow suit, and it's not long until we are alone.

"So what did you think of everyone?" Garrett asks.

"Do you want the truth?" I look at him nervously.

"Yes." He laughs.

"I hated them. Rachel was sweet, but what kind of man is she married to? She seems scared of him, and Joelle is so self consumed. Luke didn't even bother trying to talk to me, but I suppose I didn't put forth much effort. Anyways, it was terrible. Sorry, dear."

He doesn't look upset or shaken at all. "That's okay. People really are different outside of work, huh?"

I chuckle. "Movie, then bed?"

We decide to watch a TV series instead. After a few short episodes, I call it a night. Garrett is set on staying up to make sure Brynn gets home on time. I head up to our room and crawl into bed. It's not long before sleep overtakes me.

At some point I feel Garrett get into bed next to me. "Brynn is home, safe and sober."

Sunday passes in a blur. We go to church, then have lunch at home. We stay home for a few hours, then go to see a movie at the theater. It's some action superhero movie that I have never heard of. It was Garrett's turn to pick the movie. We spend the rest of the evening playing board games.

The next few weeks are uneventful. Soon enough, it will be Brynn's eighteenth birthday. She is more than excited, and just got the approval to have a large party at our house. She tells me everything I need to pick up from the store to help her set up for her party. After work I do just that. I bring home pop and snacks, a new movie, and party invitations.

"Karen and Amber want to spend the night on my actual birthday. I know it's a school night, but please. It would be so awesome."

"I will think about it." And by that, I mean spend several hours trying to convincing Garrett that it won't be a big deal, and they will be in bed at a responsible time.

Brynn and I sit and make small talk at the table, while we fill out the envelopes for her invitations.

chapter 2

AMANDA HUGH

"Momma?" Charlotte calls to get my attention. "Where do babies come from?"

"Storks, of course, honey bunny." I smile down at her.

"What's a stork?"

"It's a bird that flies around and delivers babies."

It's a warm summer day and I took Charlotte out to ride her bike in the driveway. Charlotte is four, and Rose is 1one, and I just found out I am pregnant again. Max was hoping this one would be a boy since we already have two girls. Not that he doesn't like girls; he does. I watch Charlotte ride her tricycle around the driveway until Rose is ready for a nap. I tell Charlotte to put her bike away, and we go inside. I turn on the kids channel for Charlotte to fall asleep to while Rose sleeps in her bassette. Max is at work for only two more hours, and I haven't decided what to make for dinner. I go to the kitchen and start to look for anything that Max would like. Once I realize we have nothing in the house, I pick up Charlotte and Rose and put them in the car. I manage to do it without waking Rose, and I know Charlotte will fall asleep during the ride into town. I stop at the meat market and pick up pork chops and asparagus. What should be a two-minute run into the store turns into a twenty-minute shopping trip with two children. Once I manage to get them in the car with the groceries, I start for home.

When I pull into the driveway, I nearly have a heart attack. Max is home. I haven't even started dinner yet, and I need at least an hour to finish it. I get Charlotte out of the car and have her take the bag of groceries while I get Rose.

"Charlotte, when we get inside, put the food in the kitchen and then go play in your room, okay?" I instruct her.

"Okay, mommy," she agrees quickly.

I knew a fight was coming as soon as I walked in the door. "Hi, darling. Charlotte is about to go play in her room while I make dinner. You are home early."

As Charlotte sets the bag on the table, Max barks, "Where were you?"

The slam of his fist makes me wince, and Charlotte flinch. "Honey bunny, go play in your room." Once Charlotte is out of the room I turn to Max. "I was at the store getting food for dinner."

"Why didn't you have that thought out before the last minute! What if you didn't realize until later? Would we even be eating dinner tonight? What if you didn't make it to the store?! Our family needs to eat, Amanda."

He seems to be losing his steam faster than it came. Today must have been exhausting for him at work.

"You are right, Max. I was irresponsible, and I should have made sure we had food for dinner before the last minute."

I look at the floor, waiting for his next move. To my surprise, he walks out of the room. I take the pork chops out of the bag and preheat the oven. I start mixing spices we have, and rub the product into the meat. Once that is done, I start a pan on the stove for the asparagus. I put the porkchop in the oven, and start to fry the asparagus. I add some garlic and butter to add a little flavor. While those fry, I set the table with nice dishes and placemats. I take the porkchop out of the oven, and move it over to a serving plate. I do the same with the asparagus, and place them both on the table. I get Rose and Charlotte settled in before I go get Max.

Once dinner is eaten, and everyone is happy, I send Charlotte off to play again, and Max goes out to do whatever he does. I clean up the mess from dinner and make Max a lunch for tomorrow. I bring Rose into Char's room, and read them both a book. I put Rose to bed and then go back to tuck in Charlotte.

"Mommy?" she whispers.

"What's up, honey bunny?" I kiss her head, and tuck her in.

She smiles at the nickname and then asks, "Why do you and Daddy fight so much?"

I pause for a moment and then say, "All mommies and daddies fight, bunny. Daddy just has a hard job. It makes him mad, and when he comes home he just lets his anger out. We aren't mad at each other."

"I don't like when Daddy yells. He is scary," she says sadly.

"Daddy isn't a bad guy, bunny," I soothe her.

I sit on her bed and rub my hand over her hair until she falls asleep, then I go lay down in bed and wonder where my husband is, and who he's with.

I also wonder why we fight so much, Char, I think to whoever is listening.

TWO YEARS LATER

Peter is crying from his bed, Char is ripping through her closet to find the perfect outfit for her first day of kindergarten, and Rose is still asleep, thank goodness.

"Charlotte, remember, we already picked out an outfit!" I call from the hallway on my way to get Peter.

"I don't want that one anymore!" she yells back angrily.

"What's wrong, honey?" I ask Peter as I lift him off his bed. He wraps his arms around my neck and screams into my shoulder. I carry him to Char's room to help her find a new outfit.

"This one!" she squeals, holding up her Christmas dress.

"No," I say strictly, while I rub Peter's head.

"Yes, Mommy!" Char cries.

"Charlotte, I said no. Now come on, pick something else. Your brother is hungry, and you need to eat too." I walk out of the room and place Peter in his highchair. Charlotte comes out of her room wearing the original outfit as I finish feeding Peter.

"Do you want cereal or a sandwich for breakfast?" I ask her.

"Cereal." The obvious choice.

While she is eating, and Peter is playing on the floor, I make Max eggs and bacon. I bring him his breakfast in bed; it's how he knows to get up for work now. On my way back to the kitchen, I get Rose from her bed and start her on eating breakfast. Max leaves for work the same time I leave to walk Char to the bus stop. I make Rose walk with me, and put Peter in a stroller. We walk to the end of the street to Char's stop. She has been singing and dancing the entire walk, so excited for her first day of school.

"When do I get to go to school?" Rose asks.

"In two more years," I tell her.

"What about Peter?" she pushes.

"Peter will go to school in three years," I mumble to her.

Rose starts to draw with her finger in the dirt. Normally I would scold her, but she needs a bath when we get home. Char starts jumping up and down and flails her arms when she sees the bus coming. When the bus stops, she gets on, and I watch her sit in the middle of the bus and look at me out the window to wave. Her schooling is only every other day, but not having her around three days of the week will be hard to get used to. There is nothing keeping me here in this dark world other than my children, and I don't know what I will do when they all move out and leave me alone with Max—not that he holds back now.

I take Rose and Peter back to the house. Rose is all about coloring lately, the downfall being she has been caught drawing on the wall several times. It's easy to keep her entertained so I can do housework, though. After laundry and cooking is done, I put Rose and Peter down for naps. I start dusting then, and doing dishes. Max has high expectations of the cleanliness of the house, despite the fact that we have three kids. When I go to wake Rose from her nap, I find her coloring on the wall with crayon.

"Ugh, Rose, come on!" I say, frustrated. "Do you even know how hard that is to get off the wall?"

She looks at me like that wasn't a real question. Four year olds these days. I go and get the cleaning supplies from the closet, and Peter starts crying from his crib. I pause for a moment and think, *Maybe I should let him cry it out for a moment. He won't move from the crib, and it won't take me that long to clean the crayon off the wall.* But the mother in me tells me to go get my child. I walk into Peter's room, and understand why he is crying. I almost want to cry at the smell of that diaper. I change his diaper, and then carry him to the high-chair. Rose comes out of her room looking for a snack. I get her settled, and take advantage of them both eating. I grab the supplies once again, and go into Rose's room. Just as I'm about to start scrubbing the wall, Peter starts screaming. I rush out to the dining room and find Rose shoving food in Peter's face.

"Rose, knock it off! What are you trying to do?" I yell at her.

"Sorry, Mommy," she says. "I was just trying to feed Peter."

"Well, that's not your job, and not how you feed a baby," I scold her.

She runs to her room crying. I should make her clean the crayon off the wall while she is in there. I calm Peter down, and let him finish his breakfast in peace. For the third time, I try and clean the wall off. When I go into Rose's room, she has taken the sponge and started to scrub the wall.

"Hi, Rose," I say, trying not to startle her, to let her know I come in peace. "I'm sorry for yelling at you, but you could've hurt your brother."

"I was just trying to help, Mommy," she says through tears.

"I know, baby. Thank you for scrubbing the wall." Hopefully some positive affirmation will lessen the blow of me snapping at her.

SIXTEEN YEARS LATER

Peter is graduating from school today and leaves for the army tomorrow morning. Rose just got married a month ago, and Char is now a mother and loving wife. She lives just down the road from us, and often brings my granddaughter over for me to watch while she does housework. Tomorrow is the first day of the rest of my life. I will live alone with Max starting tomorrow. He hasn't changed over the years. Instead, he's stayed just the same, an angry alcoholic who beats his wife. I've thought of killing him so many times, but I would never get away from the law. I would just be killed right after him, and I would rather hurt than never see my beautiful children again.

I was saying goodbye to Peter the next morning. Char, her husband Chet, Rose, and Auto, Rose's husband, are also here to say goodbye. We give him one last round of hugs before he gets on the bus and disappears. Char and Chet leave right away to get back to their children and work. Auto goes to start the car, and Rose turns on me. With anger in her eyes, she lets the flood gates open without warning.

"You are a terrible mother!" Rose spits at me. "You lied and kept us in the dark. We had no experience in life. How are we supposed to have any self respect for ourselves as women after you let Dad throw you around while we were in the next room? We still heard!"

"Rose, please understand." This fight has been coming for a while. Rose has been pulling away from me since she had her first daughter. I never knew the reason until she told Char last week that she despised me for not being a good mother. Rose told Char she thought I was weak, a bad role model, and not someone she wants her children to know as their grandmother.

"Understand what? That there is a reason I got sent off to private school hours away. You sent us away as soon as we hit high school. Except Peter. Why is that? Why do you favor him, Mom?" Her eyes are full of rage and hatred.

"Rose, I hear what you are saying, but I don't know what shaped your mind like this. I stayed there for you kids. I couldn't leave. We would have had nowhere to live. He would take his anger out on you, if not me." I plead with her to see my side.

She laughs menacingly in my face. "Mom, you were the one who made Dad so angry. You couldn't do your job as a mother. That's why Dad beat you."

That day shred my heart to pieces. I never thought I would get a second chance to be a mother. To do better this time, and be a good, loving wife.

chapter 3
AMANDA KRAMER (AK)

Today is Brynn's birthday, and her party is just a few days away. Brynn's friends are coming over for a few hours, but not spending the night; they do have school tomorrow, after all. Garrett gets up early and makes breakfast for everyone.

"You know what I would love for my birthday?" Brynn asks.

"What's that?" Garrett turns to look at her.

"A cat." She looks hopeful, while Garrett and I look dumbfounded.

After a few seconds of staring at each other, I say, "We will think about it."

A cat? I have never had a pet in any life. It would be interesting; in fact, I want one. Garrett can see the excitement on my face. He takes a second to think, then says, "The decision has already been made, I guess."

We all chuckle. Since we gave Brynn the day off from school, she and I immediately start talking about different breeds, and if we should go to the pet store or a rescue. It was a fast decision. We would go to a rescue. We would hope for a kitten, obviously, but love it no matter what cat we got. We work ourselves into such an excitement that we leave for the pet supplies store immediately. We pick out everything from food to a cat tower. We get treats and toys. After that, we go home and cat-proof the house, moving glass from counters, hiding cords, putting out toys and the litter box. By the time we are done, Garrett is just as excited. The three of us go to the rescue in town.

Through the sliding glass door there is a counter to the right; to the left are the rooms to play with potential adoptees, and straight ahead is all the animals. The dogs are in a separate room from the rest of the animals. We wash our hands and go look at the dogs first, just to say hi. After that, we set out on the hunt for the new Kramer family member. We find a cage of kittens immediately. Inside is one calico, one gray, and a tuxedo kitten.

"I want the calico." Brynn decides fast.

"You don't want to play with her?" I ask.

"No, she's perfect." And she was.

They put her in a cardboard cage and send us on our way. The first vet appointment is free through the shelter, and Bella Bean Kramer is added to our family just as fast as she was a thought in Brynn's head. We spend the rest of the early afternoon playing with and mostly watching Bella. Brynn makes a social media account, "Face gram" or something. She has started taking pictures, trying to get the perfect intro post.

When Brynn's friends get here they disappear into Brynn's room with Bella, but they promise not to suffocate her with attention. Garrett and I settle with a drink at the kitchen table to plan out the week's meals. Garrett does most of the cooking, so really he does most the meal planning, but that means I have to do the grocery shopping, which is exactly what I do once the list is done.

The market is busy with people bustling around. As I'm doing the shopping, I run into Mary from the firm.

"Hey, Mary!" I call out to her.

"Amanda! Hey, how was the birthday?"

"We got a cat." I laugh.

"A cat, huh? Never would have guessed that's what Brynn would want for her birthday."

"Why is that?" I ask.

"It's just most girls her age want like lingerie or something."

I would be mad if it isn't for her goofy smile that tells me she is kidding.

"Anyways, see you at the office tomorrow?" she asks.

"See you tomorrow." I wave goodbye.

I finish my shopping, get home, and put the groceries away before I tell Brynn she needs to send her friends home. I find Bella and Garrett napping on the couch with the TV turned on. I shake him awake gently, and together we head to our bedroom and crawl into bed together.

I wake up not feeling good the next morning, and think nothing of it. It's the time of year that people get sick. I walk into the kitchen and find Garrett eating leftover pancakes from last night. "Is Brynn up yet?"

"I haven't seen her," he says between bites.

I walk up to her room and knock on the door. "Brynn, are you up?"

I hear some mumbling and rustling from the other side, and then, "Oh, crap. Yeah!"

She starts hurrying around her room, then comes running out for the bathroom. I go downstairs and make her a lunch to bring to school. I get her backpack and schoolbooks neatly gathered by the door, and wait with her car keys for her when she comes flying down the stairs.

Her smile when she sees everything I've done is all I need as a reward.

"You are a lifesaver," she compliments.

I leave for work shortly after. When I walk into the office building and smell the coffee, my stomach flips circles. I run to the bathroom and throw up everything I had this morning. Since I am sick, I should go home so I don't give it to anyone else. I walk to the HR room and talk to Wanda. She tells me to feel better, and sends me on my way.

When I get home, I find Bella has ripped up the toilet paper hanging on the roll. I take the remaining toilet paper and put it in the closet. I then sweep up the shreds of paper on the ground. After the house is cleaned up from the past few days, I settle onto the couch and read a book. After a few chapters, Bella crawls up on my lap and rests her head on my leg. I lose track of time and am brought back when Brynn gets home from school.

"I'm getting a job," she states.

"Why? Where?" I ask, shocked.

"I think it would be good for me. Learn to manage my time, have some spending money, and get ready for when I have to do it in college."

"Where?" I ask again.

"The nail salon. I'm going to greet people and whatnot. Just part time a few days after school. My friend from school works there, and said I could get a job easy. They really need help." Her words say that she is telling me she is doing this, but her tone is pleading.

"Well, I think it's a great idea."

Her face breaks into a smile.

"I thought you would want me to just focus on school, and would count a job as a distraction," she confesses.

"Of course not. I think your dad will be happy you want a job," I reassure her.

Brynn's party goes by smoothly. She is overjoyed with the amount of people who show, and content with the party decorations.

I wake up each morning for the next week feeling nauseous, and decide I better take a pregnancy test. On my way to the store to get a test, I think about what it would be like to have another kid right now. Brynn is eighteen, and almost done with school. If I am pregnant, by the time the baby is born, Brynn will be living in a dorm room in college. I feel that's way too far apart for siblings to be. I mean, eighteen years? Plus, how would Garrett respond? There was a time he wanted another kid after Brynn was born. He wanted to try for a boy. That way we would each have a kid he would tease, but Brynn has always done a good job of loving us equally. If I had to guess, I would say that Garrett will be anxious for a month, and then get excited. He will go on about how he wants a boy, and complain until the ends of the earth if we get another girl; he would claim the world is against him.

When I get to the store, I go find the aisle and pick the test packet with three tests in it. After I pay for them, I waste no time, and take the first test in the market bathroom. I wait the two minutes, and look at the test.

I go home. Garrett is golfing with his friends, and Brynn is at her new job. I go upstairs to my bathroom and take the second test. Wait two minutes. Pregnant. The next thing I do is call the doctor to schedule an appointment. I am forty-five. In my last life, I had Peter at twenty-seven. I had Brynn at twenty-nine. I have no experience in raising a child when I am already halfway through this life. Anxiety takes over. My chest tightens, and I feel the blood racing through my veins. I call Garrett.

"Hey, babe." He answers on the third ring.

"I need you home. I have news." Also, I'm freaking out.

"Everything okay?" Every syllable is laced with concern.

"Yes. Just come home when you can." I rush through the words.

"I'm on my way. Give me about twenty minutes," he says, sounding even more concerned now.

I spend that twenty minutes trying to get my heart to slow down. As soon as he is through the door, I cling to him. "I'm pregnant."

His body tightens in my arms. "What? Really?"

I tighten my grip around him, not ready to look at his face. "Yes, I took two tests. They were both positive."

Now he forcefully but gently unlatches my hold on him, and searches my face for a moment, then brings me back into an embrace. "Everything will be okay. We just have another bunny on the way. I am so excited."

Those were the perfect words I needed to hear. He skipped the freak-out-for-a-month stage, because I needed him to, and in this moment, I am okay.

———

It's weeks later, and I am starting to show. I haven't told anyone at the office yet. I am going to start wearing baggy clothes until I decide how I feel about it. I don't need other people snooping around and injecting their opinions. I want my feelings to be my own until they are sorted out at least. Just as I predicted, Garrett was nervous and stressed for a few weeks after he comforted me that night, but is now excited. He talks about how he knows his sperm did a good job this time, and chose to make a baby boy. He calms my nerves about having a child so late in life. "We haven't slowed down that much," he says.

Brynn is also excited to have a sibling, even though they will be so far apart. I find out the gender of the baby at the

next appointment. We talked it over, though, and are decided on a name for each gender. We also decided that Brynn
will be the only one to know the gender, and is in charge of
planning us a gender reveal party. She also asked if she could
throw a baby shower for me down the road since we got rid
of all our baby stuff a long time ago. I told her I would think
about it. A baby shower at forty-five? I don't know.

"Mom." Brynn breaks me out of my trance. "So, your
appointment is Friday, and I have the party planned for
Saturday. How do you feel?"

"I am excited, Brynn. I'm sure it will be great." I have
always loved watching videos of baby gender reveals, and am
truly excited to see what Brynn has planned.

"Have you decided how to break the news to your
coworkers?"

The only people coming to the reveal party are some
work friends of Garrett's, probably Joelle, Rachel, and their
husbands. I told Mary and Cindy to come, though they don't
know exactly what for. I told them it was a small get-togeth-
er, just to socialize outside of work.

"No, I still haven't told them."

She makes a face. "Why not?"

"I don't know how I feel. Obviously having a child is a
blessing, and I love you dearly, but I was looking forward to
being an empty-nester again. Your dad and I have fun when

we don't have to be parents. I don't know how to feel about another eighteen years of parenting."

But now that I think about it, I could have a lot more years of parenting. Who knows how many lives are left for me; how many more marriages, how many more families. I get into another thinking trap and start to think about how mundane life can be, but it's not like there is anything I can do about it.

"Well, two of your coworkers are coming on Saturday, and I'm sure once they find out they will spread the news around. Don't you want to be the one who gets to tell everyone?" she questions.

"It might be a relief if they tell everyone. Then I don't have to. It's not that I'm not excited, I just to want to draw so much attention to it. I am older, and it's not my first kid."

"It's still a miracle of life," she says matter of factly.

I mean, she's not wrong, but it's not like I am debating getting an abortion, just my feelings. I didn't have a lot planned for when Brynn left for college, but I can't say I'm not a little disappointed.

⌒

FRIDAY AT WORK

I am sitting at my desk waiting for Mary to get done with a client. I watch her walk the client to the door and see him off. Once he is out of sight, she turns and makes a bee-line for my desk.

"You look anxious." She notices.

"I've been keeping a secret from you," I confess to her.

"What? You weren't born a natural brunette? Your color is way too perfect to be natural," she compliments.

"Thank you, and I was born a burnette." In this life, AH was blonde. "My secret is that I'm pregnant, and tomorrow is actually the gender reveal party."

I can see fireworks go off behind her eyes. Everyone but me is instantly excited about this news. "You are serious? This is awesome! How long have you known? Why didn't you tell me before? I thought we told each other literally everything, like poop count included."

I laugh at her enthusiasm, and am glad I kept it from her just to see her face now. "I don't know, I guess I just felt too old to be completely starting over. Brynn will be out of the house the next year, and it's just a lot to take in. I am official-ly excited now, though, so I decided to start telling everyone. Also tomorrow, Garrett has some terrible coworkers, and one of them has an even worse wife. So glad you can make it." I give her a fake smile.

She looks happy. "We will have plenty to laugh at on Monday then."

After work, I go straight to the doctor. Brynn is reading a magazine in the lobby when I walk in. After a few minutes of waiting, the nurse comes to get me. We go through the appointment and she seals the gender in an envelope, then hands it to Brynn.

"Should we be a good family and go home to eat with Dad? Or stop for food and shakes?"

"Compromise. Call Dad and invite him with," Brynn says.

"All right, that's fair," I mumble to her

A short while later, we are eating burgers with shakes at the diner in town.

"How was the appointment?" Garrett asks.

"I saw my younger sibling, so that's kinda cool," Brynn says.

"So far everything is fine and healthy." I beam at him.

He can sense my mood change about the baby, and by the smile on his face, must realize I'm now excited. It's hard in moments like this not to compare how much better Garrett is to me than Max ever was. Garrett can read my face and emotions like an open book, while Max didn't even consider I had feelings. It's the same way I can tell what Garrett is thinking, and what he will think of something. We just know each other, like best friends. Suddenly feeling overcome with emotion for my husband, I snuggle up to him on the booth and place my hand on his leg. We go home and spend the night watching TV. Still feeling very lovey, laying in bed, I fall asleep in Garrett's arms, though I feel him shrug me off shortly after he thinks I've fallen asleep.

chapter 4

Just like the dinner party Joelle and Luke are the first guests to arrive to the gender reveal party. "Welcome, guys."

They take off their shoes and place them neatly by the front door, bless them. They are each handed a drink, Joelle pink, and Luke, blue punch. The room is decorated in a jungle theme with plants hanging from the walls and lights, and large animals stickers on the walls. The lights are dimmed and rain forest music is playing in the background.

"How lovely your place looks," Joelle says, using big arm motions. "And pregnancy really did you a favor this time. You are just glowing."

What does that mean? "Thank you, Joelle. You look nice too." *I think.*

It's a painful half hour alone with them before anyone else shows up. Mary and her husband Bryan are the next to arrive. Mary takes one look at Joelle and gives me a knowing look. I can only start to think about how many comments she has on Joelle's makeup alone. The next to arrive is Cindy and her husband Bob. All the guys seem to hit it off right away, but there is a different story with the girls. Amber, Brynn's friend she swore I would love, is also on the guest list. When she comes in I get a very powerful feeling, though I can't identify it. By the way her face looks when we shake hands, it tells me she feels it too. Whatever this feeling is doesn't let up as long as she is around. The feeling is not uncomfortable; in fact, it's almost familiar. Even if I wanted to talk to her about it, and see if she does in fact feel this same pull, how would I go about that? "Hey, do you feel the weird non-sexual pull towards me that I feel towards you?" Not at all a weird thing to ask a teenage girl as a grown adult. So, instead I shake her hand, tell her it's nice to meet her, and try to ignore this feeling the best I can. Rachel and Josh don't show up, and I wonder if something happened.

I head to the kitchen to get a refill on my punch and some snacks. Today I chose to wear a shirt that shows of my belly, while normally I try to hide the bump. Everyone compliments me on how big I look.

"Wow, you hide that well at work!" Mary exclaims. "You shouldn't, though."

"Doesn't being pregnant look great on her?" Brynn pipes in.

I shoot her a thankful look. I appreciate all the attention, but I appreciate Brynn's a little more than anyone elses. Garrett loops an arm around me as Brynn gathers everyone for the reveal.

There is a full carton of eggs sitting on a table in front of us. Nine of the eggs are pink, and nine of them are blue. Everyone is gathered looking at us from the other side of the table. Brynn starts to tell us how this is going to work.

"You will take turns smashing an egg against your forehead. All the eggs apart from one are hard-boiled. Whichever color egg is not hard-boiled, is the gender of the baby. Blue for a boy, and pink for a girl. Simple enough," she states.

I give Garrett a sideways glance and tell him to go first. He takes a blue egg hopeful, and smashes it lightly against his forehead. Hard-boiled. I take another blue egg hesitantly, and smash it fast against my head. Hard-boiled. Garrett, getting a little impatient, takes another blue one. Hard-boiled. I take the first pink one. Hard-boiled. After a few more hard-boiled eggs, it's down to four blue eggs and six pink ones. Garrett takes another egg and smashes it against his head. The yoke runs down his face and into his mouth. He lets out an excited gagging noise and throws his hands in the air.

"It's a boy!" he yells.

Everyone cheers and starts to clink glasses together. Brynn never would tell us if she preferred a brother or sister, but I can tell now that she'd wanted a brother, and somehow it makes me proud to produce the family member they both wanted. Mary demands a family picture. Brynn goes to get Bella, and we stand smiling in front of the remaining eggs. Garrett then makes a toast, and everyone cheers again. After that, Brynn has games lined up and small gifts for the winners. We play a game of smelling the chocolate on the diaper and guessing the kind of chocolate. We played a game to test out different baby foods, and Garrett somehow wins that one.

Now it was the end of the evening. It was overall enjoyable, but definitely exhausting. After everyone leaves, we make a team effort to clean everything up. When the house is back to normal, I decide to call it an early night. Not long after, Garrett comes and lies down next to me.

"Good morning!" Mary sings happily at work on Monday. Mary never fails to be a happy person, even right away in the morning. That's probably why we get along so well. Now that I take a full look at her I notice she's cut her hair differently. She got rid of her layers and added bangs. Her red hair curls down to her shoulders; her green eyes complement her fair skin and freckles well. She is just an inch or two short-er than me, but usually wears heels so no one would even notice. She stands across from my cluttered desk. Someone walks in, and we feel the breeze from the door opening.

"Good morning," I greet the client. "How can I help you?"

"I have an appointment with Mary Gonzales," he states flatly.

"Oh, thats me!." Mary straightens out quickly and smooths her skirt, and shakes his hand. "Thank you, Mr. Conrad, for coming in. Follow me this way to my office."

She turns her back to him and gives me a wink, then leads the way to her office. The new partner was brought in a few weeks ago and has been making rules left and right. Turns out some of the rumors were true. It was the boss's bitchy wife who wanted more attention in the company. She has been running around trying to make her presence known, not that it's hard to notice her with her noisy steps and constant gum chewing. She also makes a point of announcing herself in some sort of way when she walks into a room. Charlie, the now co-partner, is letting most of what she says go, but every once in a while he will tell her to meet in "their" office.

Josh, one of the lawyers, comes to my desk. "Hey."

"Hey, Josh, what's up?" I ask.

"I just wanted to ask if you have free time today, would you fax some stuff over for me?" he asks shyly.

I give him a smile and say, "Of course."

"You are a dime, Amanda. Thank you." He gives me the papers and a thankful smile, and then leaves for his office. Not long after, his client comes in.

I look at Josh's schedule for the day and see why he asked me to fax these for him. He has back-to-back clients coming in today, and from the names I recognize, these are some pretty big cases. I make a mental note to stop in every few hours to see if he needs anything.

Charlie comes rushing in thru the front door. "Whoa, boss man, where is the fire?"

He doesn't look amused, and instead spits out, "Sarah is coming. She will be here in a few and she wants my head. Tell her I am busy with high-profit clients today and I must not be bothered. Please."

"Okay, sure, I will do what I can." He checks behind him before running to his office. Just as he predicted, Sarah, his wife, comes storming into the building not long after.

"Where is he?" she barks.

"I'm sorry, who?" I ask her.

"Charlie, obviously. Who else?" She glares down at me from her turned up nose.

"Oh, he is in a meeting with a client. He asked not to be bothered for a while. Said it was really important. Not to spoil the surprise, but he let it slip that if this case goes well, he's going to take you on vacation." That should buy him some time, and hopefully calm her down.

Normally when Sarah is in a bad mood she takes it out on everyone and anyone. Even clients at times. It's bad for business, but Charlie says if he wants to save his marriage there is nothing he can do. As sad as it sounds, why would he want to be married to someone so nasty anyway? I decide now is a good time to check on Josh. I walk to his door and knock lightly.

"Come in," he says.

"Hi." I walk into the room. "I was just wondering if you guys need anything."

Josh gives me a smile. "A smoothie would be great, Amanda."

The client asks for some water. There is a coffee shop just next door with Josh's favorite smoothies. Charlie doesn't mind that I run over there to grab orders for clients and lawyers, as long as I keep up on the phones as well. As I'm standing in line waiting to order, I feel a hand on my shoulder.

When I turn around Joelle is standing behind me. "Oh my gosh! Amanda, I thought that was you. Kate"—she looks to the girl she is with—"This is my best friend Amanda. Our husbands work together, and oh my gosh, you should see their house, so adorable."

Well, being her best friend is news to me. I wouldn't even introduce her as a friend to, well, anyone. "Hi, Kate, nice to meet you."

She shakes my hand and returns the greeting.

"You must sit with us," Joelle pleads.

"Sorry, I am actually at work right now. Just grabbing snacks for a client," I tell them.

"You are a coffee runner?" Kate asks, disgusted.

"No, I am a secretary at the law firm next door." This doesn't seem to change her mind at all, not that I care what she thinks of my job.

"Well, next time." Joelle hugs me, and they return to their seats in the corner of the cafe.

When I return, I go to Josh's office to drop of their drinks. I walk in without knocking and immediately regret it. The client is divulging some personal information that I could have lived without knowing, about his wife. I knock on the open door to announce that I am here, and hopefully stop wherever the rest of this conversation is going. Thankful, Josh rushes out of his seat to grab the drinks from me. They both thank me multiple times before letting me return to my desk. A few minutes later, Joelle comes sauntering through the front door. Great.

"Well, I wouldn't have introduced you as my best friend if I had known you were a coffee runner," she sneers, as if it is my fault.

"My bad?" *What is she even doing here?*

"Anyways, Luke would be mad if I told him I ran into you today and didn't invite you and Garrett to Jeffrey's engagement party this weekend." She looks at her nails, bored with this conversation.

"No, we have plans. Thanks for the invite, though." I turn her down quickly. I don't even know who Jeffery is.

"Thank goodness." I hear her sigh. "Anyways, bye."

She turns on her heel and walks out the door.

"Who was that?" Josh asks from behind me.

"My husband's boss's wife," I tell him.

"Seems stuck up," he comments.

"She's the worst," I add.

"Hey, thanks again for the smoothie. Best secretary I've ever had."

Even though it shouldn't mean that much to me, it does. Especially since the run-in while going to get his order.

"Josh, are you married?"

"Not after doing this job everyday," he jokes.

Josh is still young. Just out of school. He has exceled here, though, and proven to Charlie and everyone else. I think him and Garrett would get along nicely, and maybe I could set him up with one of my single friends. Is he too old for Brynn? I mean, she is eighteen now, though still in high school. Law school is long, though, so he must be mid-twenties, which is in fact too old for Brynn.

When I get back to my desk I notice someone left me a voicemail on my cell. It's the doctor reminding me that I am two years late on my annual checkup. I just hate going to the doctor and paying them so much money just for them to tell me I'm fine. Instead, I could sleep in and not rush to work, or be at home spending time with my family. I feel as healthy as I should at this age. I've gotten away with it this long enough though, so going in 1 time won't be so bad. I call the doctor back and schedule and appointment for the following week. I also get a text from Brynn asking two things: one, can we have family night and play board games; and two, can her friend Amber come? I check Garrett's online schedule to see if he has work things to do tonight. Once I am sure his schedule is clear, I text Brynn and tell her it's a great idea.

I remember the feeling I got when Amber entered the room at the gender reveal party. The force that pulled me to her. Maybe I was just being crazy, but I'm nervous to see if I will get that feeling again tonight.

chapter 5

When I get off work, I go to the store to find snacks for game night. I browse down the candy aisle and pick up some sugar chewies. I also get chocolates for Garrett and Brynn. I decide to get some soda and do a light grocery shop while I'm at the store. I get the ingredients to make tacos, and text Garrett to see if he will cook them, and what else he needs. I stroll around for a few minutes to wait for his response. He gives me a short list of things he would like. I walk around slowly, and pick up everything he asked for. I pay for the groceries, and load them into my car.

On the drive home, I find that today has really made my muscles tense up. I turn up the radio and try to relax before I get consumed with gravity from Amber again. I look out the window as I drive through the desert, cacti scattered about. I love the heat of Texas, especially compared to the cold winters in New York, but New York will always be sentimental to me. That was my first home. My only home for a whole lifetime. Something comforting and stable, before even living a life with someone wasn't enough to be forever. In my next life I think I won't get married. I already produced enough children for this earth, more than I should have the second Brynn was born. Am I messing with the future from living more than one life? Could I go and get revenge on people who wronged me in past lives, even though most if not all of them are dead? I finally decide that me having more than one life is not messing with the future at all. I am not time traveling by any means.

When I get home I notice that Brynn ripped through the kitchen looking for a snack. She didn't find any, though, because we ran out of anything flavorful last night. I unload all the groceries and put them away before I start to make dinner. Brynn comes wandering in the kitchen, rechecking for snacks.

"I started dinner already. No snacks. When is Amber going to be here?"

"She just texted and said she is leaving her house, so maybe like fifteen minutes," she tells me.

Next, Garrett comes wandering hungrily into the kitchen. "How long until dinner is ready?"

"About a half hour or so," I had expected Garrett to take over cooking when he got home but he seems to have forgotten and I don't mind doing it..

"I will start picking out a game. Brynn, wanna help?" He shuffles into the living room.

The two of them walk to the living room and debate between Risk and Dominion. Garrett prefers Risk because he would like to rule the world someday, and this helps him plan out his strategy. Meanwhile, Brynn would prefer Dominion, a deck building game. She says that Risk takes too long to play, and Amber has a curfew. I sit back in the kitchen and admire my family.

Brynn has long brown hair, to match mine, but has her dad's blue eyes. She is tan like her father, but has my height, while Garrett towers over us, with his black hair and lean body.

I finish browning the meat for Garrett before he takes over and finishes the tacos. Just as Brynn and I finish setting the table, there is a knock on the front door.

"Must be Amber," Brynn says, and goes to answer it.

I know it's Amber before she even steps in the house. The energy coming off her is just as unique as it was the first time I met her. Comforting but unfamiliar. Almost like smelling a similar perfume to the one your mom wore while growing up. I couldn't quite place what the original comforting feeling is, though. The energy doesn't get more intense as the night goes on, no matter how close or far away I am from Amber. I sit next to her at the dinner table and across from Garrett, with Brynn to my left. Brynn and Amber tell us about the school project they get to do together. They have to do a senior project to better the community in order to graduate. Amber and Brynn plan to organize a walk for fallen soldiers and their families. Each person who wants to partake will gather a team of six or more people. Each team would have a sponsor, and gather at the track and field area. Everyone would stay the night there, and one member from each team has to be on the track all night. The sponsor then donates money based on number of loops walked around the track the sponsored team does.

Their idea impresses me and Garrett, and we decide to be a sponsor for each of the girl's teams. After dinner Garrett and I clean up the dishes, while Brynn and Amber get the snacks ready in the living room. We start out by playing Dominion. The game moves slow in the beginning before everyone has a much better hand. We take turns going around, each playing our turns, and we all help out Amber, who hasn't played before. Amber ends up winning the first game, but Garrett is the first to win three total games, and is crowned the winner.

I keep catching Amber's eye, and get uncomfortable under her stare. "I will be right back."

I head down the hall to the bathroom. Once inside, I close the door and lock it. I take a towel and put some cold water on my face. For a second, I think I hear footsteps coming down the hall. When I open the door, no one is there, and when I get back to the living room, everyone is seated just where they were. Must be hearing things. After we finish playing all the Dominion rounds, we switch to playing Uno. Amber wins all three rounds, and is claimed winner before anyone else has the chance. All in all, it is a good evening, and Amber is a delight to have over. I'm glad Brynn is making good friends.

The next day starts off with a butt-kicking from my baby. I had thought morning sickness would go away at some point. It hadn't been throughout the whole pregnancy with Brynn, after all. The morning is rushed and sloppy. I end up leaving the house with mismatched socks and shoes. I didn't get a full cup of coffee, either. Everyone on the road seems to be driving extra slow as if to make me late for work too. I do make it on time, but just by the sliver of a hair. I watch Charlie watch me clock in.

"Charlie is in a bad mood today," Mary warns as he is headed this way.

"Amanda, I don't remember giving you permission to tell my wife that I am taking her on vacation?" he says angrily.

"Yes, sir, I know, I just didn't want her to keep bringing everyone's spirits down around the office, including the clients'. Maybe you both need a vacation, and even if that's only a few days off work." I rush through the words.

He sits on this for a moment before stomping back into his office. As soon as his door is closed, Mary comes slithering out from the shadows. "Way to tell the boss."

I feel the blood rush to my head at my outburst. "Maybe I went too far."

"Well, he didn't fire you on the spot, so that's a good sign," she half jokes.

"Anyway, not to take advantage of how nice you are, but I have a really full day. If I buy you lunch, would you go pick it up for us?" Her offer is more than fair, so I agree.

Just as she said, she has clients in and out all day, only taking a fifteen-minute break when I bring her food. Josh, on the other hand, hasn't had much going on today, and has been sending me memes in an email. Who knew a picture with some stupid words on it could be so funny? Josh and I eat lunch together in the break room with Cindy. Cindy's daughter is getting married, and she wants us to go to the engagement party. She says she will bring us the official invite when she gets some. Josh confesses that he normally sits with the guys, and all they talk about is sports, so he is unsure what to say. I, on the other hand, can't stop complaining about how ready I am to give birth, though I have over six months to go still. They listen to me whine with smiles on their face, as if they know my pain. I know for a fact that Josh has never been pregnant. I feel myself giving into my hormones and becoming very angry for no reason. Not wanting to blow up at someone, and make an awkward workplace for later, I excuse myself and end my lunch break early.

The rest of the day passes fast. The phones are busy, and Mary's clients are needy. It is a nice pace, though.

When I get home, Garrett is already home with dinner on the table.

"I sent Brynn to Amber's house. I took a half day at work. The house is clean, and dinner is ready."

"Thank you, Garrett. Really." I am so thankful to be able to de-stress with Garrett and not worry about Brynn for the night. She is old enough to where she doesn't ask much from us when she is home, but it's still nice to have alone time with my husband.

Suddenly overwhelmed with nausea, I lay down on the couch.

"Are you feeling okay?" Garrett asks. "You don't look too good."

He helps me onto the couch and gets my head propped up on pillows. "I feel okay. Just baby sickness."

He goes and takes care of the dishes. When he comes back, he dims the lights and lights a candle, puts on soothing music, and stands by my feets. He starts massaging my feet, and then next thing I know, I lose consciousness.

chapter 6

I wake up in the hospital. Garrett is sitting in a chair in the corner of the room, while Brynn is slumped against the wall on the floor.

"I'm awake," I say just loud enough to wake them both.

They rush to my side and both start firing questions about how I'm feeling. They tell me it's Friday morning, and that I've been out cold for the night. The doctor ran some tests, but it will take a few days to get the results back. They said all my vitals are good, and now that I've woken up, I can go home. They tell me the doctor will discuss the test results with me on Monday, and that it's convenient I already had a schedule set.

When I get home, Brynn and Garrett start treating me like I'm fragile and will fall apart at any moment.

"Guys, I'm fine. I feel fine. The doctor cleared me to come home. Stop watching me like that," I scold them, though I don't feel so great.

They both look guiltily away.

I call into work for the day, and am excited to spend the day relaxing at home by myself. I spend the day reading, and do some light cleaning. I get so bored, though, with no one around. I am excited for when two thirty comes, and Brynn will be home from school. She texts me just before school gets out and asks if Amber can come over. I tell her not today, because though I do feel fine, I am still exhausted from last night.

When everyone is home for the night, we settle into our usual routine: Brynn does homework, Garrett cooks, and I sit there and talk to both of them. Today is different; I am the center of attention with them bombarding me and asking how I'm doing. I guess the doctor told them to keep an eye on me at least until my appointment on Monday.

The weekend is long and slow. They try to be more discreet about it, but I still feel their gazes on me most of the weekend. By Sunday afternoon, I can't take it anymore, and call Mary to see if she wants to meet for dinner.

We agree to meet at a restaurant in the middle of our two houses. We get sat at a table outside and we both order a glass of wine.

"So how was your long weekend?" she asks.

"Long. Garrett and Brynn have been watching me like hawks, no matter what I say," I grumble.

"Per doctor's orders," she tells me.

"Yeah, whatever," I excuse her reasonable response.

We order our food and then settle back into conversation. "So, you missed work on Friday. Bummer for you. Charlie called Sarah into his office, and within twenty minutes, she stormed out of the building, and didn't come back the rest of the day. I hope she never comes back again."

Sarah has been hard having around the office for everyone, but she seems to be especially cruel to Mary, making comments about her outfits, and constantly down playing Mary's hard work ethic.

"Yeah, having her gone would be nice, but I don't see that happening after one fight."

"Depends on the fight." She sounds hopeful. "Anyways, how is the kitty?"

"Bella has gotten so big lately. It's sad, but she is still adorable," I say, getting excited just thinking about how cute she is.

After we finish our first glass of wine, our food arrives, and we order a second round. The restaurant is nice but nothing super fancy. The people around are dressed as if they have been having a lazy Sunday. The energy is calm and content while the employees run about. Someone at the front of the building complains loudly that their food was cold and the waitress didn't believe them. The man, who must be the manager, tries to talk her down, but ends up taking her email to send her a coupon for the next time she comes in. Mary and I both agree the woman was just looking to get a free meal. We finish our meal, pay for it, and then go to Mary's house.

She lives in a large townhouse with her husband, who is out of town on business. She gives me a tour, including the outside, then we settle on the couch to watch a movie. We debate between a soap opera or a classic chick flick to watch. Once we both agree on a soap opera, Mary makes popcorn and gets us juice. The night is spent gossiping about work, and talking about my pregnancy. She is my best friend, but I didn't know her when Brynn was born, so I promised she could be the godmother of our baby boy.

At the question Mary breaks out in tears. "Yes, of course, I would love to."

We stop watching TV completely at that point. "Why are you crying?"

I can't help but chuckle when she responds, "I've never been anyone's godmother. This is so exciting."

I feel happy knowing I just made her day, and that my boy will have the best godmother. We call it a night, and she promises to stop crying by work tomorrow.

I wake early, feeling anxious. I get the test results from the doctor today. I have felt mostly fine since Thursday night, but still a little off, and definitely tired. I get ready for work more slowly than normal. Maybe I should drink an extra cup of coffee today to get me going. Brynn comes down the stairs happily.

"Good morning, Mom," she sings.

"What has you in a good mood so early?" I ask her.

"I don't know. Today is just a good day. Plus, you get cleared from the doctor and find out the fainting was nothing. Then I don't have to keep watching you," she teases.

Even if she didn't like watching me, there is no way she is more excited for them to stop keeping on eye on me than I am. Everything today moves slowly, traffic, work, even the walk to my car and into the office building seems longer than normal. When I reach the doors, Sarah comes flying out with an armful of her stuff. Guess Mary was right. It does just take the right fight. Sarah gets in her car and drives away without a look back. When I settle into my desk I thought I had better go check on Charlie. This could partly be my fault by suggesting that they take a vacation together. Well, I did more than suggest it. I told Sarah that it was going to happen. What if that's what the fight is about? Charlie didn't want to take her anywhere, and now they go in a big fight about it. Things would be weird between me and Charlie, knowing I was the one who ruined their marriage, or at least put a dent in it. I walk to Charlie's office door and knock.

"Sarah, I told you not to come back!" he yells.

I crack open the door and poke my head in. "Sorry, boss, just me."

He looks relieved and waves me in. "What can I do for you, Amanda?"

"Actually, I was here wondering if I could do anything for you? I saw Sarah storm out, and even if I didn't, the way you just yelled tells me something is up. Care to share?" I try to be casual.

He contemplates the idea for a moment before asking me to sit down. "I suppose if I were to talk to anyone, it would be you. When you told me we should take some time off and spend time together, I realized I didn't want that. I want to be at work because I can't stand her. I'm getting old and tired of work, though, too. I need somewhere to relax, and that just wasn't home anymore. So I told her to pack her stuff and move into the house in Florida."

He doesn't seem that upset about it; in fact, he looks a little younger now. "Well, I'm glad my advice helped, even if not in the way I thought," I joke with him.

He smiles at that and nods. "Thank you."

"No problem." I get up from my chair and walk back to my desk.

Just a few seconds later, Mary is at my desk. "So what happened? You always do that thing where you check on people to make their days better or easier. You did that right, and he told you everything that happened with Sarah?"

Always looking for gossip. "Yes, that is oddly exactly what happened, but it was a private talk, and I can't tell you anything he said. Just know you will have a much better time here, because she is not coming back."

"Oh, so they are getting divorced. Too bad it would be a conflict of interest for me to be his divorce lawyer. I would get a firsthand look into all the drama in their love life," she says with a wicked grin on her face.

After work, I go straight to the doctor for my appointment. The waiting room is mostly white, with white couches. A large desk is in the front of the room with three cubes to get checked in at. I walk to the open one on the left.

"Hi, how can I help you?" A girl smiles at me from behind the counter.

"Hi, I have an appointment. The name is Amanda Kramer," I tell her.

"Date of birth, Amanda?" she asks in a polite tone.

"May 30, 1974," I tell her quickly.

"Perfect, I got you checked in. They will call you from the right side," she says, and points.

I go sit on the side she pointed at, and look through a magazine. I watch a lady with a walker come in, check in, and go sit on the left side. Within minutes, someone is out to get her. Her name is Tami. Ron is the next one to be called, a large man wearing a gray shirt, jeans, and outside work boots. I watch as more people get called back, and start to wonder if they forgot about me. Just as I'm about to get up and ask if they did in fact forget about me, a short blonde girl comes and calls my name. I stand up and go meet her by the door.

"Follow me this way," she says, and takes the papers the lady at the front desk gave me.

She takes my height and weight, then walks me to a small room with three chairs in it. She takes the chair at the computer, and I sit against the wall.

"How have you been feeling since you fainted on Thursday?" she annoyingly asks.

"Tired, but I haven't been sleeping well. Other than that, I feel great," I tell her patiently.

She goes over a few more administrative questions before going to get the doctor. When the doctor comes in, she shakes my hand and introduces herself as Doctor Anderson. She goes over some of the admin information again, and I get the feeling she is stalling.

"Doctor," I say, "how did the test results come back?"

She takes a pause, looks at the nurse, then says hurriedly, "You have aggressive breast cancer. Unfortunately, you have less than six months to live, and you will most likely lose your baby."

My world stops. I have only had eighteen years with Brynn. That isn't enough. I thought I was supposed to live full lives. How can an Amboi get cancer? Why didn't I get the symptoms, or know this was happening before? On top of that, she said I would lose my baby. I will die before he is born, and he won't have a chance. Nobody in the room moves, speaks, or dares make a sound breathing.

"Thank you," I say, and get up to walk out of the room.

They try to ask me to stay, or come back in for another appointment, but I don't hear anything. Just because I get reborn when I die doesn't mean I wasn't enjoying this life. I love Garrett and Brynn. I have the perfect, loving family, with the perfect job. How could this happen? I am not ready to mourn my family, and I'm especially not ready to become part of another family.. When I died the first time, I was happy when I found out that I got to retry life. Do it better, and I did do it better. This time, though, it feels like a neverending circle, or a broken record.

When I get to my car I take a few minutes to do some more processing of the information before I start the engine and drive home. When I walk in the door, Brynn and Garrett are nowhere to be found. Now that I think about it, Garrett will be home any minute from work, but that doesn't explain where Brynn is. I go upstairs and run a bath.

I let the hot water loosen up my muscles and try to relax. Never in a million years did I think that would be the results of me faiting. Eventually Garrett finds my pruned body in the bath.

"How long have you been in there?" he asks.

"Since I got home from the doctor." My voice sounds dead, even to me.

"Bad news?" I can tell by his tone that he doesn't have a clue as to how bad.

I start sobbing and pull myself out of the tub. "I have cancer. I am dying, Garrett, and the doctor said I would most likely lose our baby in the process."

I know the news will hurt him just as bad as me, if not worse. He not only loses his unborn child, but also the only wife he has ever known. Telling Garrett was the relatively easy part. Telling Brynn is the hard part.

chapter 7

I text Brynn to see where she is. She says she is at Amber's, and will be home late. She asks what the doctor said. I tell her there is nothing to worry about for now. I don't know how to tell her about the cancer, but I do know that a text isn't the way. Garrett and I spend the night going over different scenarios with Brynn and how she might react. We roleplay until we have it memorized how we want to tell her. I wonder if I had gotten cancer in my old life, would my family, other than Char, have even cared?

Death in my old life was easy. Rose wasn't talking to me; Peter made a career out of the army and was never around; and I wanted nothing more than to get away from Max. Even if that meant death. I had started to lose my mind in old age, hardly able to recognize friends from the nursing home. I would hear nurses talking about me and how my alzheimer's had gotten so bad they had the same conversation with me everyday. It didn't bother me much at the time, or even now. I know I had lost my mind, and I felt myself give away in the end when death came for me. It was peaceful in the night, and I made a smooth, painless transition into the Amboi world, but I have seen what cancer does to people. It makes them sick, and their last days miserable. It destroys their body and mind, and it will destroy my family as well.

I fall asleep crying into Garrett's chest while I feel his tears soak my hair. I don't comment on it, though, knowing he wants to be strong for me right now.

The next morning, Garrett isn't beside me when I wake up. Instead of going to the kitchen for coffee first thing in the morning, I avoid it as long as possible. I'm not avoiding the coffee, or the kitchen, I'm avoiding Brynn. We said we could call her into school if she asked, but we couldn't keep this secret from her anymore. We decided last night that we would tell her this morning. I brush my teeth and take a long shower, then I do my hair and makeup. I get dressed for work, then reluctantly go down to the kitchen. Brynn is seated at the table eating an omelette, while Garrett is standing at the oven making another one.

"Good morning," Brynn says, sounding nervous, as if she knows something is wrong.

"Good morning, honey bunny." I kiss the top of her head.

"So what's with the gloomy mood this morning?" she asks.

This is it. The time for the talk. Garrett finishes his omelette and takes another out of the microwave. He sets one in front of me, and sits down with the other. We look to each other for confidence, and then I begin.

"Brynn, yesterday I told you a white lie. The doctor didn't say I was okay. I didn't tell you then because it wasn't appropriate to tell you over text." Suddenly, I can't remember a single word of the speech Garrett and I came up with the night before.

Sensing that I don't know what to say, Garrett takes over. "Brynn, your mom has aggressive cancer, and doesn't have long to live. The doctor gave her about six months."

We decide not to tell her about me losing the baby at the same time. Let this sink in, and we will tell her when it happens. The shock and concern is clear on her face. She tries to hide it, but the tears escape.

"You should've told me to come home last night," she says through sobs. She gets out of her chair and comes to wrap her arms around me. "Mom, what am I going to do without you?" She cries into my chest.

Listening to her cry makes me cry, and soon we are a mess of a family, all crying in a huddle in the middle of the dining room. Brynn does not go into school today. She said she couldn't handle it after the news. I, however, do go into work. I would like to keep this life as normal as possible until the last possible second. I want to be strong for Brynn, and let her know how much I love her, and I want her to know that she won't be alone, and that Garrett can love her enough for both of us. I know, though, that telling her these things won't make her feel them. Like Mary told me in the breakroom, "Knowing it in your head is different than feeling it in your heart." I spend the day thinking about what Brynn will do in the future. I tell her she should be a teacher. She is so good with kids and has so much patience. She never showed much interest, though. She has always exceled at the musical things, like choir and band.

I feel it's only fair to let Charlie know that my days here may be numbered, that way he can find a replacement and have me train her in before my time is over. I should also tell Mary and Cindy the news. Mary will be heartbroken, and probably won't leave my side the rest of the time I'm in this life. She will shower me with attention, and always be available when I need her, and be there even when I don't want her to be. That's the great thing about Mary, though, and why she is my best friend. She is loyal to the ends of the earth, and the most open-minded person you can talk to. Yes, she likes her gossip and drama, but it's all in good fun.

It's funny how when you know your life is over, you start to reflect on it. I guess I get to reflect on two lives. I also get to wonder what my next life will be like, or is this the last one? That's a scary thought in itself. When is my last life? Could this be it? What if I don't wake up in the Amboi world? What if Amogny isn't the one to greet me when I open my eyes for the first time in the afterlife? I try to avoid people as much as possible, but Mary and Cindy hunt me down on my lunch break. Probably a good thing, since I need to break the news to them.

"There you are. I was starting to wonder if you were even here today. Your desk has been empty all day."

"I have cancer. My days are numbered, and I won't be here much longer," I blurt out, because I don't know how to put it any other way.

They both look shocked, and try to gauge if I'm joking with them. Once I break out into tears and convince them I'm not, they both start crying as well. We all go into the family restroom and lock the door. We sit on the bathroom floor in a circle, and I spill my guts.

I tell them about fainting, which Mary already knew about, and about being so tired lately. I never imagined it would be cancer, though. I tell them about Garrett finding me in the bath, and the talk we had about telling Brynn. I cry the hardest when I tell them about the look on Brynn's face, and the sadness that immediately took over. It was the saddest face I had ever seen in either life. It broke my already shattered heart. I tell them about the meeting with Charlie, and even give into Mary needing gossip, and tell her about the fight that Charlie and Sarah had. To attempt to lighten the mood, she thanks me for getting rid of the she devil.

Once we are done with our sobbing party in the bathroom, we take turns freshening ourselves in the bathroom mirror, then return to work like nothing happened. I guess I should start thinking about quitting instead of just waiting until I can't work anymore. Though I want this life to be as normal as possible, it would be nice to have time off.

The doctor calls me as I'm leaving work and asks if I can come in. They made a mistake with the results, and would like to talk to me in person about the changes. Hopeful, I tell them I can be there in twenty minutes. I call Garrett and tell him the news. He offers to meet me at the doctor's office, but I tell him not to bother. I am hopeful that it's good news, and I can tell him when I get home afterward.

I speed, excited, to get there. After I walk in, I check in and go to sit in the same spot I sat on Monday. After just a few minutes of waiting, the nurse comes to get me. She takes my height and weight, then leads me to the doctor's room.

She asks me the same general questions she did last time before leaving to get the doctor.

When Dr. Anderson comes in with the nurse, I get concerned. That doesn't look like the face of someone bringing good news. Instead it looks like the face of someone bringing really terrible news.

"Hi, Amanda. I'm sorry about this. We hardly ever get a wrong diagnosis—well, not diagnosis. Sometimes time is hard to judge. At first look, we thought you had about six months to live. When another doctor took a look at it, he noticed some things we didn't. Unfortunately, it lessens your time with us," she says not too sadly.

"How long do I have?" I ask, on the edge of tears. Maybe Garrett should have come.

"Three months. At most," she whispers this time.

Again, unable to process, I get up and walk out of the office. This time they don't try to call me back, or offer treatment plans to help me be more comfortable. They just let me leave. I call Garrett as soon as I get in my car.

"Hey, honey. Good news?" he asks, just as hopeful as I was before walking into that room.

I hate to break his heart, and I'm sure he can hear me break out into sobs. "Garrett, they messed up in a bad way. I only have three months left." There is no response on the other end. "Garrett?"

"Yeah, I'm here, Amanda. Wow. It's just a lot to process. I'm sure you aren't having any easier of a time than I am, though. Can you drive? Or should Brynn and I come get you?"

If I can get my tears under control, then I will be fine to drive. "I will drive home. I just need a minute first. I'm going to get off the phone now. I will see you in a little bit. Goodbye."

"Goodbye, see you in a bit," he says, and I hang up.

I take a minute to collect myself and wipe away my tears, then I set off for home. When I walk threw the door, Brynn throws her arms around me.

"I'm sorry, Mom," she whispers in my ear.

I hug her tightly back for a moment, and then let her go. Dinner is ready, and we sit down to eat, but no one says anything. No one can speak. The weight of the news is too much. The cancer hasn't been known about for more than a few days, but already it's making my family grow distant. I won't let that happen this time, though. Last time I never fought for Rose to stick around. I was too scared and I just let her leave. I won't let Brynn or Garrett just leave, though.

"How was your day at home, honey? Did you get much homework done?" I ask Brynn.

"Um, no," she confesses.

"I can help you after dishes are done, if you would like." We all know I'm not the parent who is good at helping with homework, but I can tell she appreciates the offer.

"Sure, Mom, I would love that." She beams at me.

chapter 8

Since the cancer has shortened my life—well, this life— more than imaginable, Garrett and I decide to take a long weekend and spend the whole day Friday together. The week passed slowly, with everyone giving me sad looks at work. Mary did spread the news, and I decided it was too much to continue working there. I put my two weeks in that Thursday, and left feeling like a light weight was lifted from my shoulders. I promised Mary and Cindy that I would make time for them in the next couple weeks, and have a girl's night as a last hurrah. It makes me sad that I have to plan days like these at all.

Friday morning didn't come fast enough, but eventually it came. I wake that morning feeling better and more well rested than I have in the past couple weeks. Garrett is still snoring beside me. I decide to get out of bed and go make coffee. I get the paper and start to read through it. When I finish my first coffee and the paper, I go and turn on the TV.

I hear Brynn come down the stairs and into the living room. "Hey, Mom."

"Good morning, Brynn." I get up and follow her into the kitchen.

We sit at the table while she eats cereal before school. "How do you feel?"

She asks me every morning. "Good," I tell her.

She looks at me unconvinced, but says nothing.

"Any big plans after school?" I ask her.

"Nothing special, just going with Amber and Kelsey to a movie." She sounds bored.

"That should be fun. You were right about Amber, by the way. I like her." She perks up at that.

"See, I knew you would," she says proudly, as if she made me a friend instead of herself.

At least I can leave this life knowing that Brynn has good company. When she leaves for school, I go and wake up Garrett.

"Oh, shoot, honey, I slept in on our special day." He is too sweet.

"It's okay. Brynn just left for school and is going to the movies after. We have plenty of time," I reassure him.

He looks as if he is going to fall back asleep for a second, then gets up to take a shower. "Give me twenty minutes I will be ready."

We don't have anything planned today. We are just going to see where the Texas air takes us. We start by going out to breakfast. We go to the local diner. Garrett drives, and I get lost in the thought of what it means to be an Amboi. I know I get multiple lives, and that no one can tell me how many, but what if it's hundreds? What would I do with a thousand lives? Do I have other powers? No, Amogny said we are just like humans. He also said that we would get some sort of sign from the universe that our lives are numbered. I don't think I've gotten any kind of sign. Or what if cancer is a sign? What if me getting cancer is the sign of my last life? I mean, Amogny only said it was rumored, so what if it isn't fact because no one can confirm it? Holy shit. Is this my last life? I mean, I only lived two. I guess two is better than one, and definitely better than hundreds. Should I be spending these last days of Amanda Kramer's life as the last of Amanda the Amboi life?

With this new revelation, I decide I should in fact live as if this is my last life. Though this revelation also brings a new kind of sadness. Losing my family is one thing, but I've gone through it before. Just like dying. I was planning on being born again to a new family; the blow of cancer was lessened because of it. Now, though, with this possibly being my last life, cancer is just as hard on me as the next person. I suddenly break out into tears. I am dying for the final time. I am losing my family and leaving my daughter without a mother. She is only eighteen. She still needs me. Garrett still needs me. They have to not need me, though. As much as I suddenly want to fight and stay alive, I know that no matter how hard I try, I can't win this fight. I cry harder and harder until Garrett pulls into the parking lot of Sparky's .

"How can I help?" he asks, on the break of tears.

"I am dying," I spit angrly. "I am only forty-five. How can I leave you and Brynn? How can I leave? It's not fair."

By now he has pulled me into him as much as he can in the car. He rubs my hair and kisses my head as he whispers reassuring words. It isn't enough, though. "Can we go home?"

"Of course," he says, and puts the car into drive.

I mumble on about how it isn't fair the whole way home. Garrett makes us breakfast and we settle into comfortable silence. I sit at the dining room table and watch him cook. He looks so cute the way he scrambles eggs. His muscled body leans over the pan in concentration, so as not to burn them. His dark hair is slightly gelled on his head, and his brown eyes are fixed on the pan.

"You're cute," I tell him.

"Why?" He blows me a playful kiss.

"You just are," I tell him, and he accepts my answer.

When breakfast is almost done cooking, I get a candle and a fake flower to make it romantic. I turn the lights off and set the table. He serves us food and then sits across from me.

"Bon appetit," he says with a flick of the wrist.

I chuckle at him, and eat some food.

"So how was work this week?" he asks me.

"Slow. Everyone kept looking at me as if I was going to drop dead any second. I know it could be soon, but they don't need to walk on eggshells. Also, I put in my two weeks yesterday."

He gives me a surprised look. "How does that feel?"

"Good." I smile. "I'm planning to see Mary and Cindy a couple days after I'm done there."

"That sounds like a fun idea."

"How was your week?"

"Good. Also went by slow," he comments.

"What are you thinking right now?" I ask him.

"What are you thinking?" he fires back.

"Not fair. I asked you first." I defend myself.

"Yeah, but I want to know more," he attacks again.

"Fine." I surrender. "I was just thinking about how good this food tastes."

"Promise?"

"Yes. Now what are you thinking?" I ask again.

"I was thinking about how long we have together," he almost whispers.

"Garrett." I want to comfort him like he did me, but I just don't know how.

I can't tell him everything will be okay—we both know that would be a lie—so I settle on the lamest, blandest thing and say, "I love you."

He can tell I don't know what else to say, and tells me he loves me back. When breakfast is done, we do dishes together. He rinses, and I put them in the dishwasher. We don't talk, because neither of us knows what to say.

After dishes are done, we have to decide what to do next with out day together. I have no ideas.

"How about bowling?" he suggests.

It doesn't sound fun, but there are no better ideas. "Sure."

This time we make it inside the building before I have a breakdown. I wouldn't say it is a break down. I just need a minute to collect myself in the bathroom. Who knew I would be so sentimental about my last time bowling? Pregnancy hormones don't help, especially coming from a baby I won't even have. We get our bowling shoes and pick out our balls. We haven't gone bowling together since a double date in high school with my brother. Is that why he brought me here?

"Why did you suggest bowling?" I ask him, paranoid.

"I didn't have any better ideas. Did you?"

"No. Just curious." No need to bring it up and ruin the mood.

After three frames, Garrett is in the lead, but only by five. I decide I need a little help pulling ahead, and surprise him with bumpers. I get a spare, and he tells me to turn the bumpers off. He is up to bowl the fourth frame. I sneak up behind him, but not too close. He walks up to throw the ball. As soon as it leaves his hands, I run up and step over the foul line.

"Hey, that's cheating!" he yells, not mad.

"Well, you didn't let me use bumpers!" I yell back, faking anger.

"Yeah, 'cause that's also cheating!"

"Well, you are just mad because I'm winning now," I say, sassy, and go to grab my purple bowling ball.

I make sure he isn't behind me when I throw the ball down the lane. In the end, my tactics work, and I win the game. He now has to buy me fruit snacks as part of our bet. We may be childish sometimes, but we have fun. Garrett makes me laugh more than anyone has. Even in my past life. He is so outgoing and free-spirited, it's hard to be in a bad mood around him.

"Garrett, what do you think about Mary and Cindy?" I ask him.

"That's out of nowhere. I like Mary. She is a good friend for you, and very nice." He only partially answers the question.

"And Cindy?" I push.

"Well. She is weird. She is too quiet, and honestly makes me uncomfortable." He looks uncomfortable just telling me this.

It's hard not to laugh. "What? She makes you uncomfortable because she is too quiet?"

"Yeah."

"Interesting" is all I can say.

Next, we decide to go on a drive. We don't know where we are going, but we aim for an hour drive. We take turns picking songs and singing along the way. We stop halfway at a gas station for energy drinks and snacks. I get jerky, while Garrett gets chocolate. When we finish our drive, we end up at a large mall. We do some window shopping before finding a mini golf course lit by blacklights. The theme of the golf course is SpongeBob, with crooked wooden signs pointing us in the right direction, and glowing cacti. The course is outlined in glowing green lights. The walls are covered in cartoon flowers and blue water. We pick out our clubs and different-colored balls. I go with purple, again, and Garrett goes with blue, again. We go through them quickly, and this time, Garrett wins the bet, and I owe him a beer.

"What we do next is a tie-breaker for our events today. A fight to the death is in order," he says.

"Well, what would that next activity be then? No fighting or death involved," I tease him.

"We shall hail to our homeland and have a cook-off. Brynn will be the judge."

"Not fair! You know you are a way better cook than me. Let us have a drawing contest."

"Inconceivable!" he says in an accent, quoting *The Princess Bride*. "We shall have a battle of wits, and try our hand at chess."

I laugh but agree. Being that we don't even own a chess board, we go to the store and get one. When we get home we both have to read how to play multiple times, then begin the game. He goes first, and then me. We take turns, and kill several of each other's pawns. He takes out my horseman with a bishop. I fire back and kill his bishop with my other horseman.

"Dang. Didn't see him there." He defends his play.

"Always have a backup plan, babe." I say as if I planned it.

"So what does the winner of our contest today win?" he asks.

"Well, I should get a small prize for beating you in chess since the other two parts, the winner got a prize, and for the overall prize, I think you treating me to a makeshift spa day at home would do."

"All right, I will agree to those terms. Winner gets a makeshift spa day at home, and a small prize for winning in chess." He doesn't trash-talk back, but makes sure I know he isn't out yet.

In the end, I am the winner. He might have let me win just to treat me to a spa day, but that's why I married him.

The spa day starts when the chess match is over. He cooks me a light dinner and starts the bath while I'm eating. He gets all the things gathered for a pedicure and sets out a towel. When I go into the bathroom I see he's set out a robe, bath bomb, facial mask, and razor for me. I chuckle at the razor. I sit down into the bath. Perfect temperature. I set the bath bomb in water and play with it using my feet. I put the face mask on, then wash my hair. I use the razor while the conditioner sits. According to Garrett, I must have really needed to shave my legs. Once out of the bath I take my time to dry my hair and put the robe on. Garrett is waiting for me in the living room. I sit on the couch and he starts to take off my chipped nail polish. I stop him and tell him I will paint them later when he starts to paint side to side, instead of up and down. After he finishes the pedicure, he gives me a massage and plays with my hair. Brynn gets home while we are laying on the couch, my head on his lap, watching a movie.

"Aren't you guys cute?" she comments. "Anyway, I'm going to my room. Have a goodnight, love birds."

When it's time for bed, he gives me a small refresher back rub, then pulls me into his arms.

"Today was perfect," he says, and kisses my head.

"I wouldn't trade it for the world." I tilt my head towards his and kiss his jaw. We fall asleep laying like this.

The next morning I wake up and shower. I go downstairs to find Brynn finishing yesterday's homework at the dining table. "Do you need help with that?"

"Sure. I'm having some trouble writing this paper."

I sit with her for an hour, and we finish her paper. Brynn is an excellent writer, but she has some trouble getting going. She just needs someone to inspire her. I'm glad I can help her with some homework at least. I have always been good at English, but fall short in math and science. Good thing Garrett is so well rounded, and can help her with everything I can't. Speaking of, I should see where Garrett is. When I walk into our bedroom, I hear our shower running. I think nothing of it until I hear a crash against the wall.

I run into the bathroom. I can tell right away that the sound was Garrett's fist connecting to the shower wall. "Garrett, why did you just punch the wall?"

The tears are hard to see with the water from the shower mixed in, but there is no denying his swollen red eyes.

"I can't parent without you. I can't be both of us, Amanda. As hard as I try, your absence will also be noticed on holidays and birthdays, our anniversary, and your birthday. Brynn's wedding day. When she graduates high school." He is full on crying now.

"Mom, is everything okay?" Brynn calls from outside our room.

"Yeah, Brynn, we are just talking!" I yell back to her. I turn back to Garrett with a soothing voice, "Honey, I know it will be hard, but if there is anyone who can do it, I know it's you. I am so sorry you are put in this situation, and if I had a choice, you already know what it would be. Just be strong, Garrett. I will be watching you. Keep that, and think of it when you need strength. Time will help, I promise. Things will get better. They just have to get a little worse first."

He takes a moment to let the words sink in, and then responds, "I love you, Amanda, and no one could replace you. I just want you to know that."

I can't have this conversation with him right now. I need to be the strong one, comforting him, and if we go down that path I will be the one needing comfort. "I love you too, Garrett."

The rest of the weekend, and the rest of the week, goes by fast, and the next thing I know, it's my last day at work.

chapter 9

I am four months pregnant, with two months left to live. My daughter graduates high school in five months, and I would be celebrating my twenty-first wedding anniversary in four months.

I walk into the office for the last time to find everyone gathered around my desk with a cake. It says We Appreciate You.

"Thank you, guys." I try my hardest to smile at them.

There is no way today could be a good day. In fact, it's hard to imagine anymore good days, with what's lingering in the near future. While everyone is getting cake I tried and escape to the bathroom. Mary is watching me though and follows.

"Whats up?" she asks.

"Just not in the mood to celebrate, you know." My voice sounds sad even to me.

"Yeah, I know what you mean. I tried to tell them not to."

"I would've thought you'd be the one to plan this," I half tease her.

"No. I know this is hard on you, and every time you think about it must be another stab in the chest."

"Exactly." How she knew exactly how I felt when I didn't, is beyond me, but I'm thankful for it.

We sit in the bathroom together for a few minutes before Cindy comes to get us. I tell Charlie I'm not feeling well, and would appreciate if I could leave early. He said he doesn't mind, and walks me to the door.

"Sorry if the cake was too much. We were just trying to do something nice," he explains.

"I know, and I appreciate it, but my death isn't something I would really like to draw attention towards," I snap. "Sorry."

He doesn't look hurt, just understanding. "It's okay. Go home. I hope you feel better."

I drive home with the music on loud. It isn't enough to drown out my thoughts, though. I turn the radio to a horrendous rock station, and turn it up loud. Now that's enough to confuse my mind enough to stop thinking.

When I get home, Brynn is in the living room.

"Why aren't you at school?" I startle her.

"Oh, um . . . " She looks like she is about to lie before telling me the truth. "I was having a bad day. Too much is going on, and I needed a break from life for a day. No one would be home—or so I thought."

"I'm not mad, but you should've texted me first. I would've come pick you up for ice cream."

"Next time." She laughs. "Now, why are you home? Shouldn't you be at work?

"Yeah, they threw me a party, so I had to get out of there."

"They threw you a party?" She is clearly shocked at the idea.

"Well, I mean, they had a cake, and they were gathered around my desk when I walked in the door, so does that count as throwing me a party?" I ask her.

"Not your usual party, but we will count it this time," she tells me.

I yell out in pain.

"Mom, are you okay?!" Brynn rushes to my side.

Blood is pooling around me, and I yell in pain again. "Bring me to the hospital! And call your dad."

I try to breathe as if they are contractions, but they aren't. The pain is firefly, and wild. It consumes my body. Brynn gets the car keys and helps me into the car, then dials Garrett's number and gets into the driver's side. Once on the way, she tells Garrett that I am losing the baby, and to meet us at the hospital. Funny how the hospital is the farthest thing away in this city. It feels like a lifetime before we finally make it. As soon as we walk through the door, the receptionist goes to get help. Two nurses come rushing my way. One of them gets me settled into the wheelchair and pushes me, while the other one starts firing questions at me and Brynn. Garrett arrives just as they have me in a room. When the doctor comes, he has Brynn leave the room.

I can tell Garrett doesn't know if he should be with me or Brynn right now.

"Stay with me," I plead him.

When it's over, I spend the night in the hospital. Garrett and Brynn go home for the night and promise to be back for me first thing in the morning. The nurses check up on me every few hours to see if I need anything. It's nearly midnight when I hear the door open, and I close my eyes to pretend and be asleep. They put a tray on my nightstand, then leave the room. I open my eyes and find an apple with some orange juice and crackers on the tray. I'm not hungry, but eat it anyways.

When it's over, Garrett and Brynn go home for the night. I had to spend a week in the hospital to recover. When I finally get to go home, Brynn is the only one to pick me up from the hospital.

"Where is Garrett?" I ask her.

"At home. I told him to stay. You and dad had a whole day together, and today is my day with you. Dad and I can spend every day alone together the rest of forever—please, not, but if we really wanted, we could," she states matter of factly. "I know this week was tough on you, but today I have planned."

The first stop is the hair salon. Though Brynn is the one who drives me here, Garrett gave her his credit card to pay for it. Brynn tells me I can change my hair however I want, but suggests a short bob. The hair stylist agrees, so it's a done deal. She takes her time and chops my hair off. I always hated having short hair, but my long hair has a been a mess lately. Once she finishes, she tells me not to look in the mirror because it isn't the end of my makeover yet. She takes me over to the hair-washing station and sits me down. I tilt my head back, and she places hot wax around my eyebrows. Over one spot at a time, she places the wax, covers it with a white cloth, and then rips it off my face. Ouch.

Now that my hair and eyebrows are redone, I can look in the mirror. I hardly recognize myself. I have lost weight around my face, and no longer have a baby inside me. Though I like the change, it's hard to be happy about. I will only look like this for two months at most before my body starts to decompose. It feels like a waste of time and money to be getting myself dolled up.

"Hey, Brynn, don't you think this is kind of pointless? I mean, with me about to die and everything. It just seems like a waste of time and money," I explain to her.

"Mom, it's for you to relax. We have all had a long, hard couple months. This isn't just for you, it's for me too. I promise the rest of the day isn't so 'wasteful,'" she says, begging me to go along with the next activity.

"Okay. What's next?"

She doesn't tell me, but instead takes my hand and pulls me into the car. We are off and driving again. Well, only across the street to the nail salon, I guess. Brynn already made us an appointment, so when we walk in, they are ready for us. We pick out our colors, and then go to rest our feet in the hot water. One person is doing our toes and feet, while another is doing our fingernails.

"Thank you, Brynn," I tell her.

My head is leaned back against the chair and my eyes are closed. I didn't get much sleep last night, and this is the perfect position to nap. The nail salon employees keep up a steady conversation with us, though, so it doesn't leave time to sleep. When we are done at the nail salon and back in the car, Brynn turns to look at me.

"We are going to go home. By both dad and me, you are ordered to do nothing but relax. You have a massage appointment at five"—in three hours—"and that's the last thing you have today," she tells me.

"Thank you, Brynn. Today was very relaxing, and I appreciate the thought, honey." I squeeze her hand.

When we get home, Garrett has lunch made for us: grilled cheese, with tomato soup. Yum. We all sit at the table after grabbing plates of food.

"How was your girls' day?" Garrett asks.

"Not over yet. Mom still has a massage," Brynn informs him.

"It's been very relaxing. Thank you for paying for all that, dear," I say to him.

He smiles at my thanks. "No problem."

When lunch is over, I go up to my room and lie down. I try to fall asleep before my massage in a few hours.

I know I am dreaming because I am in Amboi HQ. Amogny is there sitting on his throne beneath the archway. There are four lights above him. The first light is burnt out, the second one is dimly lit, the third and fourth lights glow brightly.

"Welcome back," Amogny greets me.

"Hey." I wave to him. If this was real life, I wouldn't be so casual towards him.

"Hey?" he questions. Can he come and talk to me through dreams? No, that would be crazy, right? I mean, he isn't even on earth. I wipe the thought from mind, at least for now.

"Yeah, it's how some people say hi or hello. But hey," I reply.

"I know what it means. It's just so casual," he comments.

"Well, if I can't be casual in my dreams, where can I?" I retort.

"Well said. Anyway, how is Amanda Kramer's life going? Almost over. That's a bummer, but better for me." He laughs menacingly.

"Why would that be better for you?" I ask, now scared.

"Well, because then I get to eat your soul." He laughs loudly now.

I wake up in a pool of sweat. That wasn't a dream, it was a nightmare, and I would hate to see Amogny look like that in real life. I would, if he ever got mad. I mean, he is the Amboi leader, who helps Amboi transition into their new life and teach us what it means to be an Amboi. I can't see that being very infuriating, but what do I know?

It's almost four thirty now, and Brynn will be coming to wake me any second.

Before she comes to wake me up, I meet her in the kitchen. "Are you coming with me? Or is this a solo mission?" I ask her.

"Solo mission, sorry. I am finishing homework. Gotta stay at the top, ya know?"

Brynn is at the top of her class, and so far will be the valedictorian, but she says there is a boy named Thomas who is really close to beating her GPA.

I grab the car keys off the counter, and leave for my appointment. When I check in, they tell me that Garrett has already paid for it. He is so good to me. It's just a short wait before the masseuse comes and gets me. She introduces herself, and then leaves me alone to get undressed, and under the covers. A few minutes later, she knocks on the door, and then enters. She mixes in a smell with the lotion, and begins on my legs. Brynn was right when she said the day wouldn't be so wasteful. This massage feels amazing, and the haircut isn't half bad. The makeover helps pull me out of my funk, and I no longer see the end so bleakly. Yes, it doesn't make me live any longer, but I have faith that this isn't my last life—it was all in the lights.

chapter 10

Friday morning, I sleep in and rest. I notice I sleep a lot better through the nights, but don't feel rested in the morning. Garrett and Brynn have already left for work. I go downstairs and make a pot of coffee. While the coffee brews, I turn on the news. They show terrible weather in the northern states, and how schools are shutting down. They talk about snow, and I remember the New York winters.

They were harsh and bitter. The cold would instantly nip at your nose and cheeks. When the snow came fast, the plows would take a while to get out on the roads, and the sidewalks were often slippery and full of snow. If you had to go anywhere, you had to leave extra early to make it on time, and were often redirected because of a crash or too many cars in the ditch.

The day goes by fast. I spend most of it reading and watch TV. When Brynn gets home, Amber follows.

"Hey, how was school?" I ask them.

"Good," they say in unison, and then go straight to Brynn's room to do homework.

"Good talk," I say to myself.

A few minutes later, Garrett gets home from work.

"You are home early."

"Yeah, boss let us go early for doing good on a project this week," he says with glee.

He appreciates the small things in life.

"Well, that will be fun to have a few extra hours tonight," I comment.

"Yeah, I look forward to it. I will come back down and entertain you after I change out of my work clothes." He rushes up the stairs, and comes back down a few moments later.

"That was fast. I should start calling you Garrett the Lightning Bug." I laugh.

He chuckles at my expense, and says, "The lightning bug? They aren't even that fast. They get their name from glowing in the dark."

"Yeah, yeah," I say dismissively.

We settle on trying to play chess again. We spend the night together sometimes playing games, and sometimes drinking and talking. Brynn and Amber are up late before they go to bed. Just after they turn the light off, Garrett and I lie down for bed ourselves.

Saturday morning, Garrett makes waffles for everyone. I make the coffee, while Brynn and Amber set the table. They also take a frozen concentrated apple juice out of the freezer and mix it with water. We eat breakfast and chat about everyone's day.

"We are going to go to a school play at seven tonight, and today we are just working on our school projects. Just real plain jane," Brynn tells us.

Garrett and I are meeting with Mary and Bryan, Mary's husband, for a double date. Cindy was not allowed to be there, according to Garrett, and Bryan quickly agreed.

"What is with these guys and Cindy?" I ask Mary.

"Bryan doesn't like her 'cause she is so boring, and never does anything. What about Garrett?" she asks me.

"He said she is too quiet, and makes him uncomfortable." I laugh at the memory.

We go to a nicer restaurant, but still not the fanciest around. Sitting at the table, we scour our menus. None of us have been here before. It's a Mexican restaurant, and has a very authentic menu. Not being very hungry, I just get chips and guacamole. Garrett gets taquitos, and Mary and Bryan share a large burrito. They all get alcohol, but ever since I got pregnant, alcohol hadn't appealed to me, which means I am the permanent sober driver.

"What do you do again, Bryan?" I ask him.

"I am a landscaper. I plan the layouts of people's yards for them, draw it up, and give it to the team." He seems excited, talking about his job. I bet he likes it. When dinner is over, I feel exhausted. We head straight home, and I call it an early night.

Sunday goes by fast. I mostly sit around the house trying to regain energy. I play multiple games of chess with both Garrett and Brynn, and we make a tournament out of it. Brynn wins the tournament undefeated. Who knew she was so good at chess? I take a nap in the middle of the day to prepare for movie night. We watch a comedy we all haven't seen yet. Garrett and Brynn love the main actor, while I typically don't like his films, but I agree to watch it since I am outnumbered. It ends up being funny, and I am glad that I was open minded and watched it. We all go to bed early, Brynn in preparation for a long day at school, Garrett ready for a hard day at work, and me simply because I'm exhausted again.

⌒

I am feeling more hopeful today than I have in weeks. I get up, shower, and do my hair and makeup. I go downstairs and make everyone breakfast. When Brynn and Garrett make their way into the kitchen, I have bagels and cream cheese set out on the table, with coffee made and pancakes. I also added some fruit to make it look like we are healthy, but I know they won't touch it. We eat in silence, but enjoy the meal. When they leave for work and school, I sit in the living room with a book. I lie on the sofa against the back wall, with the loveseat to my left, perpendicular to me. The TV sits on a large wooden entertainment center, and we have a brown wooden coffee table. There are red couch pillows on the loveseat, one with an *A*, one with a *B*, and one with a *G*. The living room is next to the dining room, which leads to the stairs, entryway, and bathroom. Up the stairs and to the left is Brynn's room; straight ahead, another bathroom; and to the right, is the master bedroom, with a master bathroom connected. Our house isn't very large, but it's perfect for our small, tightknit family. I take a few more moments to appreciate the home we built for ourselves before deciding I need to get out and do something.

I go to the sports store and get some rollerblades. I spend an hour and a half rollerblading in a park not too far away. After I get tired out, I sit on the bench and watch some of the people skate around. There is a young couple, about mid-twenties, holding hands and skating together. There is trio of men racing around the rink shoving each other when they pass. I spot a young woman with a small child, and start to pay attention to them.

"Come on, honey," the mom coaxes her daughter. "You can do it."

She gives her daughter a walker to hold on to as she learns to balance on her own. "Yay, Mommy!" the young girl cheers as her mom moves around her.

She moves in front of her daughter and crouches down and calls to her daughter. "Come on, Sadie, come to Mommy."

The little girl listens to her mom and slowly rollerblades over to her.

When I get tired of watching, I go to the local pool and sit under an umbrella. I have lost too much weight to be in a swimsuit anymore, and all my clothes are baggy on me. I pick a spot out the of the way. I watch little kids have swim class and yoga class going on in another pool. In the public pool there is a game of water volleyball going on. The team closer to me is winning, but from what I see, not by much. I watch the volleyball game until the team farther away from me pulls ahead and wins the game.

When I finally go back home, I am completely wiped. I start a bath. I begin lighting some candles around the tub when I hear my phone ring from the kitchen.

"Hello?" I answer, knowing it's Brynn.

"Hey, can Amber come over? Her parents are fighting, and she can't go home right now. Don't tell her I told you. She would probably flip out and be super mad at me," she rushes to say.

"Um, that's fine, but when?" I ask, concerned for Amber's home life.

"Well, she will be here any minute. Also, I have student council, so I will be home in about a half hour."

Great, she is leaving her friends for me to entertain. I understand where she is coming from, though, and I wouldn't want to send Amber home to fighting parents. I would rather she be here safe. I hang up the phone, and am about to walk upstairs, when the doorbell rings.

"Hey, Amber, come on in," I greet her.

"Hi, Amanda, thank you. My parents are fighting, and I just can't deal right now."

"That's no problem. You are always welcome here. I hope you know that." I try to push a strand of hair behind my ear, but it's too short and just falls back into place.

We walk into the living room and turn on the TV.

"How is your day going?" she asks, like she's trying to make small talk.

"Oh, good. I went rollerblading and to the pool today," I say proudly.

"Wow! That's very active and outgoing for you," she commends me.

"Thank you. It felt good to get out, and who knows how much longer I will be able to go out and do things like that," I say sadly.

"Try not to think about that. Try to think about a bucket list, and crossing things off, achieving goals, and having a positive outlook on life, no matter how short."

"Those are wise words. I will do what I can to remember them," I praise her. "Would you like to play a board game?"

She seems anxious, and I just wish I could calm her nerves, and am glad when she agrees. We settle on playing Sorry. It's a mindless game, and we settle into easy conversation.

"How was school today?" I ask her.

"It was good. Long, though. I have so much homework, and I have no idea even where to begin," she says frantically.

"You could stay here tonight, and Garrett would be more than happy to help you. He always helps Brynn with her homework, and I know he wouldn't mind."

"If you don't mind, that would be awesome!" she exclaims. "But I would like to go to the bathroom and call my parents to ask if that's okay."

"Of course. The one down here is terribly dirty. Use Brynn's. Up the stairs, straight ahead," I instruct her.

"Thank you, Amanda. All the support you guys offer me means the world to me."

She walks up the stairs, and I hear the bathroom door lock. I can hear her conversation, and can tell that she has to try hard to convince them. I hear her start to cough in the background, and wonder if I have cold syrup.

The next few moments happen too fast to react to, but slowly enough where I can see everything that happens. Smoke rolls down the stairs and covers the front door; the flames are quick to follow. On first instinct, I get out of the house. I make it, slowly, across the street. It then hits me that Amber is still in the house. The gravity that I normally feel is weak and distant, though I know I'm not that far from Amber. I quickly think over my options. I can call 911, and leave Amber to the flames, or I can run in there and risk my short life and try to save her. As soon as the thought is in my mind, I am already running back towards the house. I push open the front door and get on my hands and knees. I heard when you are in a fire you should stay low to the ground, so that's what I do. I slow-crawl up the stairs and hear Amber call out for help. I crawl to the outside of the door and try to open it. Locked.

"Amber, it's Amanda. Can you open the door?" The flames have eaten my bedroom apart, and aren't far from turning the bathroom she is in to dust.

"I can't see through the smoke!" she yells as loud as she can, and it hardly gets to me.

"Feel your way to the door. I know you can do it. Stay low to the ground!" I instruct her.

I feel her start to move behind the door. Soon enough, the door opens slowly. I take her hand, and we crawl towards the stairs. When we get halfway down the stairs, a beam from the ceiling falls, and cuts off the rest of the way down. What now? We have both breathed in too much smoke to go back up the stairs. This was our only exit. We sit on the stairs and breathe in the smoke freely now.

"Are you an Amboi?" she asks me.

"Yes. Is that what this is? Have you ever met another Amboi before?" The only possible explanation as to why she knows what an Amboi is, is because she is one.

Before she can answer me, the flames swallow us up.

BRYNN

THAT MORNING

I wake up for school, and go to shower. Today I have a test in almost all of my classes. I took all advanced classes to try and stay at the top of my class. Amber is in most of my classes, so we do all our homework together. When I get downstairs, Mom is sitting at the table with bagels, cream cheese, and coffee. I don't know how she drinks that stuff so much. It's sad to see the way the cancer has taken over her body. She has lost weight, and is skinnier than I have ever seen her before. Her cheeks are almost sunken in, and her eyes aren't so full of life. I notice she has placed out some oranges and apples. Does she expect us to eat that?

Dad comes down not too long after, and we eat breakfast as a family. I typically enjoy my time with my parents, especially now that Mom doesn't have much longer. Even when she was healthy, though, I never wanted to do anything they weren't okay with. I realize I'm not as outgoing and wild as most high schoolers. I sit at home most nights and do homework, or play games with my parents. It's a simple life, and I appreciate not having all the drama other kids in my class do. All they have on their minds is the opposite sex. Honestly, dating in high school is overrated. I would rather plan for my future, and work to get into a good college. I haven't told my parents yet, but I think I would like to major in math, though Mom always tells me I would be a good teacher. Numbers have always appealed to me. There is only one right answer, and it doesn't leave you second-guessing on every question. Unlike English. Every question has thousands of answers, based on who you are and how you perceive things.

I leave for school and spend my first hour, study hall, preparing for next week's assignments. I get a good head-start on next week's homework before the bell rings and it's time for my math test. I feel confident going into it, but feel less than confident leaving the room afterwards. I thought I was prepared for the test, but I just didn't understand some of the questions. I decide I will follow up with my teacher, and see if he graded the tests after school.

"Hey." Amber finds me by my locker.

"Hey," I greet her back.

"Can I come over after school? My parents are going at it again. They try to bring me into the middle of it every time, and my dad already told me he was going to be at the bar all day," she says nonchalantly, but I know how much it hurts her.

"Of course! My parents would love to have you over," I reassure her.

I know my mom loves Amber. They are so much alike it would be hard for her not to like Amber. I noticed how my mom took a liking to Amber the very first time they met. At the gender reveal party, Mom kept glancing at Amber, and would smile largely when I would catch her.

"Thanks, and tell your parents thank you also." Amber smiles at me.

"No problem," I tell her as the bell rings again, and sends us to class.

At lunch I sit with Amber, Kelsey, and Taylor. The spring dance is just around the corner, and the lunchroom is alive with nerves. Everyone is wondering who is going to ask who, and who will be crowned dance royalty. The most popular kids always get crowned. Year after year, Samantha Keller and Jason Hut win, and every year, everyone wonders who will win. All the girls sit around, anxiously waiting for their knights in shining armor to come ask them to the dance. Their problem is that they never leave their pack of friends to even give the poor guys a chance to ask. Lucky for me, everyone knows I don't go to school dances, so don't bother to ask.

Today after school, the student council will be putting up posters announcing the theme for the dance, and spirit week leading up to it. Kelsey and Taylor are also on the student council, and I am the student council president. I only did it to make my college resume look good. I don't actually like the school activities, and never go, I just have to plan them all. I let the student council members who actually go make most the final decisions. I do more supervising, and give advice when needed. No one seems to mind, though.

"How are the spring dance preparations coming?" Amber asks us.

Kelsey, being the most excited about it, launches into detail telling her what we have planned out so far. "So awesome. We are doing an underwater theme for the dance. The week leading up to it is Disney-themed. Monday is *The Lion King*; Tuesday, *Robin Hood*; Wednesday, *Sleeping Beauty*; Thursday, *Snow White*; and Friday, the day of the dance, is

The Little Mermaid. We are going to have the place decorated like Atlantis, and have mermen and women painted on
the walls! Ugh, I'm so excited! And guess who already asked
me to go with him? You will never guess. Trevor Lang!"

She is out of breath by the time she rushes through everything. She has also had a crush on Trevor Lang since the
beginning of the year.

"Oh, wow! Congrats!" Taylor tells her, truly excited.

"How did he ask you?" I ask her.

"We were sitting in history, and he passed me a note that
said 'Will you go to the spring formal with me?' And there
were two boxes, one with yes, and one with no. I obviously
checked the yes box, of course." She laughs.

Amber laughs too. "Of course."

We eat lunch quickly, and then go stand by my locker
to talk.

"How is your mom doing?" Kelsey says barely above a
whisper.

The topic is sensitive, but they ask once a week just to
check in. "She is doing okay. She doesn't look too good, and
has stopped working now, but she is still doing things."

Amber meets my gaze and gives me all the comfort she
can with just a look. I give her the most thankful look I can
muster. I try not to lean on my parents in this time, because
I know they are taking it just as hard as I am. Every night I
cry on the phone to Amber and tell her how much it hurts

to know my mom won't be around when I graduate. Life is unfair.

"A child is supposed to outlive their parents! Parents are supposed to guide you through life, but how is my mom supposed to do that if she isn't here?!" I shout in my head.

The rest of the school day passes fast. It's the end of the day, and I'm standing by my locker. I wait for Amber to come talk to me before I have to leave for the student council meeting.

"Let your mom know I am on my way," she says behind me.

"Oh, shoot, I forgot to ask her, but she will be fine with it. I will text her now, and see you in about an hour," I tell her.

"Sounds good." She waves goodbye, and walks out to the parking lot.

Little do I know, this is the last time I will see her alive.

At the student council meeting I instruct people to break into pairs and put up the posters for the dance around the school. Once people are paired up, I tell each group which area of the school they have. Taylor is my partner, and we have the lockers in the main area. We tape posters on every few lockers, and make light conversation as we go.

"I wish you would go to the dance," she says. "I mean, you put so much time and effort into planning it. You should enjoy it too."

"It's hard to enjoy things like a dance with my mom at home," I say bleakly.

"Oh, sorry," she mumbles.

"No need to apologize. Things have just been hard lately." I try to make her feel better.

"I understand," she says shortly, and that's the end of conversation.

When all the posters are up, and the meeting is over, I stop at my locker to pick up my bag. I then text Amber and let her know that I am on my way, and she doesn't have to suffer alone with my mom much longer. I walk out to my car and get inside. I put the car in drive and pull out of the parking lot. My car isn't very nice; my parents bought it for me on my sixteenth birthday, and it wasn't new then either. It's nicer than most of my friends' cars, so I can't complain. I stop for gas on the way home, and get snacks for a long night of studying with Amber.

Police cars and fire trucks go zooming by the gas station, and I hope that no one got hurt. I finish paying for my gas and snacks before leaving for home.

The road is closed, but I can see the lights from where I am. Is that my house? I park the car on a side street and start to sprint towards home. The police have it taped off. There isn't much of the house there. I see an ambulance parked close by, and the lights are off. Hopefully that means no one needed it. When I get closer, a police officer approaches me.

"Sorry, ma'am, this is closed off," he says, as if I'm dumb and can't see that.

"This is my house," I tell him.

"The man who lives here said it's just him, his wife, and child," the officer says, confused.

"Yeah, I'm the child." This makes him more confused.

"Oh my God, Brynn!" I hear my dad yell.

I run over to him, and he wraps me in a tight hug. "Dad, what happened? Is everyone okay?"

His face grows dark. I didn't notice the tear stains on his cheek before. "Dad, what happened?"

"Your mom . . . " He can't finish, and doesn't need to.

"And Amber?" I ask.

"They found two bodies, Brynn. I thought it was yours," he says through sobs. "We also lost Bella."

I lost my best friend. I sent her here. This is my fault. It's then that I break out in tears. I was supposed to have more time with my mom. Not much, but today wasn't the day. She was happy this morning. I saw her smile while we were eating breakfast. This isn't fair.

"How did the fire start?" I ask my dad, my voice harsh.

"They don't know yet," he tells me.

Sooner than I would've wished, they tell us we will have to find somewhere to stay for a while, as if we couldn't figure that out. We don't have any family around.

My dad takes us to a motel, where we sit and stare at the ceiling, not knowing what else to do. Eventually I hear him start to breathe deeply, and know that he fell asleep. I get out of the motel bed, and walk outside. The motel is in the middle of town, and I could walk anywhere from here. I start to walk. I'm not sure where, but I need to get out of here. I text my dad in case he wakes up, and let him know not to worry, I just needed to clear my head a little.

The news of the fire spreads fast. Kelsey and Taylor have been trying to call me for hours now. I don't have the time or energy to talk to them, though, so I keep sending them to voicemail. Kelsey's name comes up on my phone again, and I decide just to turn it off. I walk around for what feels like minutes, but when I get back to the hotel room, it's nearly four in the morning. I lay on the hard bed and close my eyes, trying to fall asleep.

At some point I must have fallen asleep, because the sun coming through the window is what wakes me up.

"Morning," Dad says sadly from his bed.

"Morning." Normally I would get out of bed, shower, and then go see who is downstairs, but today there is no one else, and there is no downstairs. There is no mom with bagels, or Amber to be my rock in this hard time.

They told us that we could go back to the house today. The house is gone, and in its place is nothing. Nothing like what runs through my mind; nothing like what I see when I look into my dad's eyes; nothing like what I feel where my heart should be. A police officer meets us at the house and tells us that mom had candles lit in the master bathroom, and

Bella must've knocked them over, causing the fire. The candles had been burning for a while before Bella knocked them over, meaning Mom was most likely distracted trying to get Amber's mood up. She was always good at soothing people and knowing when they need it. It's like her sixth sense, and I know how upset Amber was leaving school. They said nothing made it out of the fire, and we had to start completely over.

This was the end of Brynn, who had two loving parents, and was top of the class. Brynn, who had the perfect life, with nothing to complain about, to suddenly being Brynn, whose mom and best friend died in a tragic fire. Brynn, who now only has a father to act as both parents. I know this is going to be hard on Dad, but it's hard to think of anyone else's emotions right now.

We stare at the burnt-down building for a few more minutes before I go to school. Dad took the day off to get our life back on track. He was going to go house shopping, grocery shopping, and even get us new clothes.

Everyone at school has heard the news, and gives me even more sad looks than they did when they found out my mom had cancer. This town is too small to keep anything to yourself. In every class, the teacher asks me to stay late to see how I am doing. All the attention gets old fast, and I do the only thing I can think to do, and skip the rest of the day.

I go out to the parking lot and unlock my car. When I get in, I turn the music up louder than I ever have, and let it take over. I let it control my mind, and lose my feelings in the song. It's only a tap on my window that breaks me out of this trance.

It's Taylor. I roll the window down only a touch, not looking for company.

"Hey" is all she says.

"Hey."

"Mind if I sit with you and break my eardrums too?" she teases.

Because she doesn't ask how I'm doing, or if there is anything she can do to help—she doesn't even ask to talk about anything—I let her in the car.

Just as she promised, we sit in silence, listening to the loud music. I lay my head back against the headrest and close my eyes. When the song ends, I tell her I should probably go back to my motel room before a teacher finds me out here. She gets out without a word, gives me a small smile, and walks back into school.

chapter 12

SIX MONTHS LATER

It's summer. I should be happy, but it's Mom's birthday. She would be forty-six today. Since the fire, we moved into a new house in a new city. We couldn't stand everyone around constantly staring. I drove the extra miles to school every day, and it was worth it. Since school ended a month ago, things have been quiet and nice. I finally have time to deal with everything that has happened. I have started going to therapy weekly. His name is Jared, and he is great. He seems honestly interested in what I am telling him. He isn't taking notes during the appointment, and doesn't need a refresher of the week before every time I come in. It's nice to have someone I can open up to, and almost lean on, without getting a sad look or an offer to help in some way. He just sits there, listens, and tries to help me figure out what to do next, and sees how I feel. I have also started medicine for the depression that followed the fire.

Dad, on the other hand, hasn't dealt with it at all. In a way, I lost him that day too. He lost himself in work, trying to get past the pain. He still hasn't, though, and I have yet to have more than a five-minute conversation with him. Kelsey was too intrusive, and kept pushing herself on me. Eventually I had to cut ties because she was so overbearing. Taylor has stood quietly next to me, holding my hand the whole way through. She is there when I need her, and backs off when I need the space, even if it's for a week at a time. She doesn't take it personally. She lost her dad when she was younger. She said she doesn't remember it happening because she was so young, but she knows the pain of only having one parent. I often spend nights at her house, and have gotten to know her family well. She has a younger sister named Abby, and an older brother named Keith. Keith isn't around much, though.

Overall, things have settled into a new normal. It's not ever going to be as good as the normal I remember, but I'm thankful for the time I had with my perfect family.